The black hole of the barrel stared hungrily at its target

Bolan was holding the Beretta 93-R at arm's length in doubled fists. It was pointed at Bleeder's forehead.

It was a judgment from heaven and hell.

"In here, April," Bolan said. She entered with the Wilkenson Arms Linda semiautomatic pistol gripped in both hands like a submachine gun.

"There's no one else around," she said.

"Just us chickens," Bolan said to Bleeder.

Something broke inside the guy. "How'd you get in here?" Bleeder croaked.

"We busted your door down, that's how."

"Who are you? Cops? Where's your warrant?"

Bolan looked at him long and hard. "I'm about to perforate your lungs with it, guy," he said.

Mack Bolan stabs at the heart of the frustration and hopelessness the average person feels about crime running rampant in the streets.

—*Dallas Times Herald*

Also available from Gold Eagle Books,
publishers of the Executioner series:

Mack Bolan's
ABLE TEAM

Mack Bolan's
PHOENIX FORCE

MACK BOLAN

THE EXECUTIONER 57

BOLAN

Flesh Wounds

A GOLD EAGLE BOOK FROM

W♦RLDWIDE

TORONTO • NEW YORK • LONDON • PARIS
AMSTERDAM • STOCKHOLM • HAMBURG
ATHENS • MILAN • TOKYO • SYDNEY

First edition September 1983

ISBN 0-373-61057-2

Special thanks and acknowledgment to Ray Obstfeld
for his contributions to this work.

Printed in Canada

"Other sins only speak, murder shrieks out. The element of water moistens the earth, but blood flies upward and bedews the heavens."

—*Daniel Webster*

"This is the twentieth century, and civilized men will not hate the savages. Yet we cannot allow the savages to have their way. I believe I understand why I am here, even if most of the world does not. The savages cannot be allowed to inherit the earth. Why defend a front line thousands of miles away when the real enemy is chewing up everything you love at home?"

—*Mack Bolan*
(from the Vietnam journal)

Dedicated to the seven military bandsmen
killed by a terrorist bomb while
performing in Hyde Park, London.

1

The tall beefy man in the plaid lumberjack shirt snatched the half-full beer bottle by the neck, smashed the bottom on the edge of the bar and pressed the jagged glass against Mack Bolan's cheek.

Beer trickled down the man's thick hairy wrist. Most of it was sopped up by his shirt-sleeve, the rest dripping onto his steel-toed boots. A couple of splinters of brown glass were stuck in the back of his hand, drawing blood like slurping mosquitoes. But the burly man did not seem to notice.

The guy stretched his upper lip into a sneer that revealed large slabs of gray teeth, and his nostrils flared, revealing a forest of wiry black nose hairs.

He took a step closer, pressed the shattered bottle deeper into Bolan's cheek. It was not enough to break skin, but enough to send most men home in need of a change of pants.

Bolan stood calmly with one foot on the brass railing, an elbow resting on the scarred bar top, a mug of beer gripped in his right hand. His eyes were bright as flares. He gazed into the bigger man's grizzled face.

"You break it, you buy it," Bolan said softly.

"Huh?"

"You broke my bottle, pal, and there was still half a brew in it. So this round's on you. Understand now?"

The big man looked confused for a moment and Bolan realized the guy was just not used to anyone talking back to him. Ever. Bolan could see why. The red plaid shirt barely concealed the mob of muscles crowded under the worn clothing. The thick mustache and beard hardly hid the twitching sneer of his mouth.

His craziness was drug induced, Bolan could tell. Benzedrine, maybe. The way the pupils had dilated, he'd probably already popped three or four today. And it was not yet noon.

"Hey, Grayson," the bartender said soothingly. "The fella didn't do nothing. He was just standing here drinking a beer—"

Grayson shook his head violently, still maintaining the pressure of the broken bottle against Bolan's cheek. "This s.o.b. is up to something. Been following me all day. Seen him at the hardware store. Then at the supermarket. Saw him buy a pack of cigarettes at Tina's. Now, Pete, you know I always buy my cigarettes at Tina's, dammit. Always." Saliva foamed on his lower lip, dribbled down his chin. He wiped it away with his dry sleeve.

"Hell, Grayson," said Pete, "*everybody* in Susqua buys their smokes from Tina. Christ, I got a machine over in the corner and even *I* used to buy from her before I quit. Now put that bottle down before I call Sheriff Dobbs. He'll boot your ass in jail again for sure.''

"Son of a bitch has been following me, I tell ya!"

Pete looked uncertain as he studied Bolan's face from across the bar. The three other men in the bar also studied him from their table. "You been following Grayson, mister?" Pete asked. Grayson continued to press the broken bottle against Bolan's cheek.

"I wasn't following anybody." Bolan sipped his beer without moving his head. The slightest shift would cause the sharp teeth of the bottle to shred his cheek. "I went to the hardware store to buy some film for my camera. I went to Tina's to buy cigarettes. I got an ass-numbing drive back to Philly ahead of me. Simple as that.''

"I checked his car, Pete," Grayson said. "Filled with camera crap. All kinds of scopes and stuff.''

"How about that, mister?"

"I'm a photographer," Bolan muttered. "Trees and streams. Birds. That kind of thing. Tweet, tweet.''

Bolan could see there was going to be trouble. The backwoodsman started to rock back and forth on his feet, the heavy boots crunching broken glass, grinding it into white powder.

"He's all right, Grayson," Pete said. "Leave him be.''

"Fuck you, Pete. I know what I know. And I know Byron will want to hear about this guy.''

Pete's face went stony. The other men shifted uncomfortably, fussed with their beer and cigarettes. "You just forget about Byron York and the rest, Grayson. That's not for you. Besides, they already tossed you out on your butt. Forget those people."

Grayson spat, just missing Bolan's shoe, then sneered: "They'll think again when I bring them this little pecker. Come on, asshole. We're going for a ride."

Bolan glanced at Pete out of the corner of his eye and realized that neither he nor the other men at the table were going to try and stop them. That was good. If they did, the first casualty would be Bolan's face. And his face had surely been punished and beaten and surgically tampered with enough in his lifetime.

Besides, he had already decided: he was not going anywhere with this drugged-out clod.

"C'mon!" Grayson insisted, grabbing Bolan's upper arm, keeping the jagged edge of the bottle biting against Bolan's cheekbone.

"Okay, okay," Bolan said. "One last sip and my time is yours."

Grayson snorted. "Your *ass* is mine, jerk-off."

Bolan sipped a mouthful of beer, turned to face Grayson and sprayed the beer between his lips into Grayson's eyes.

Bolan ducked under the arm that wielded the broken bottle, considered snatching the Detonics .45 from its specially rigged ankle holster but abandoned the idea. He was supposed to be a nature photographer, not a gunman.

Instead of drawing his gun, he pivoted, grabbed the hand that held the bottle, then yanked it tightly under his arm. Using his own forearm for leverage, he pressed down on Grayson's wrist until it snapped like a stick of kindling.

Grayson howled with rage. Bolan grabbed his beer mug from the bar and whacked it across Grayson's cheek.

The bones in the guy's face collapsed. Skin split along the cheekbone. Thick blood bubbled out.

Grayson staggered back a couple of steps, beyond pain because of the amphetamine pumping through his veins. He reached into his muddy jeans pocket with the hand that still worked and pulled out a heavy pocketknife.

A flick of the wrist brought the blade out with a click as it locked into place.

"Enough, man," Pete warned him. "Enough."

Bolan backed up against the bar, felt the wooden edge press against his spine. He waited.

"Grayson, drop it," Pete pleaded. "This fella knows how to handle himself."

But Bolan could see that talk was useless. Grayson was not listening. He heard his own tortured voices, benzedrine voices that urged him onward.

"Son of a bitch," he mumbled, and charged.

Bolan spun away from the clumsy maneuver, slipped to the side, and with a repetitive movement of fierce speed and force, dug his elbow twice into Grayson's ribs. The ribs caved in under the attack.

Grayson sagged to his knees, gripping the edge of the bar for balance.

Bolan stood behind him and slammed two sharp punches into the back of the man-mountain's head.

Two hundred fifty pounds teetered, then collapsed onto the dirty floor. The floorboards groaned; a pillow of dust feathered up around the unconscious body.

Pete walked around the front of the bar, drying his hands on his apron. He stared at Grayson. "Guy sure as hell had it coming, but I never seen anyone able to deliver it to him before."

"Lucky punch," Bolan said.

Pete shook his head. "We should all be so lucky." He prodded Grayson with his toe. No movement. "Guess I oughta call Sheriff Dobbs over in Treetop. Shouldn't take more than an hour for him to get here."

Bolan made a show of checking his watch. "An hour for him to get here, another hour of questions. I really don't have that kind of time. I must get back to my darkroom if I'm going to make any money out of this trip."

"Suit yourself, mister. I can't quarrel with anyone making an honest buck."

"Fine." Bolan stepped over Grayson's snoring body and headed for the door.

"Hey, what about that last round of beer?" Pete called after him. "And the glass?"

Bolan nodded at Grayson. "He broke it, he bought it."

Bolan left the bar and jogged down the narrow street to where he had parked his Fury II sedan. He could tell before he got there that the back door had been tampered with.

He cupped his hands around his eyes and pressed his face against the tinted glass. The back was empty. The three cameras were gone. The satchel of spare film, the telephoto lenses, everything.

He wasted no time looking over his shoulder. He jumped into the car, twisted the ignition key, jammed it into gear and stomped on the gas.

One thing was certain. They were onto him.

2

For the tenth time, Bolan glanced around the interior of the moving Fury and wished he'd made Grayson eat that pocketknife. While the slashed seat covers and missing cameras were irritating, the theft of the negatives had flushed hard days of recon down the tubes. But to return to Pete's place would only draw more attention, or the police.

Bolan was a pro. He could walk away from the negatives, but that did not mean he liked it.

Recently there were a lot of things he didn't like. He had always trusted his own keen judgment and hard-won skills rather than any expert or any expensive toy that the government had to offer. He wanted to be free of the government.

Now, his judgment told him that a trail of trouble began with the bloated speed freak who had trashed his car. Grayson and the bartender had mentioned a Byron York. To Colonel John Phoenix, that name had an odd ring of familiarity.

At the wheel of the sedan, in the slanting evening light, Bolan's face softened. He allowed himself a small smile. At least the first set of negatives had gotten through to Stony Man. Experience again, he told himself; never stash all your negatives in one place.

Bolan speed-shifted down a flat stretch of road between two hills. At dawn he would rendezvous with Brognola at an arranged spot in the Alleghenies. Static on the car radio cleared as the vehicle escaped the hills' interference. The sweet strains of Willie Nelson's "On the Road Again" poured out of the driver's window. April's favorite, Bolan thought. Then, as quickly as the radio had found its signal, an unpleasant thought surfaced. Why had Hal, and not April, answered his latest scrambled phone call to Stony Man?

Bolan picked up speed as the song faded into the now-dark hills. He had called Stony Man Farm only minutes earlier, using a roadside pay phone that he had fitted with a portable scrambling device. He had asked Hal to keep an official eye on Grayson. Hal had responded by arranging their upcoming meeting, then reporting that the negatives relayed earlier from Bolan's motel had shown a clue as to the whereabouts of the man Stony Man was seeking.

But Bolan had wanted to hear April's voice, had expected her to answer. She was back at her job after convalescing from wounds suffered in Italy in the Laser Wagon hit against Paradine, and indeed she was evidently anxious to get into high gear. Bolan had hoped to hear her voice as confirmation of her complete recovery.

He thought about the beautiful woman who had reintroduced him to the good place inside himself that might otherwise have died with the women of his family in Pittsfield, when his personal war began. The image of his mother was clear, as always, but it was his sister Cindy who really stood out in his memory. In many ways April reminded Mack of Cindy. Like Cindy, April had been a nice girl whose ideas about the world were decent and generous and basically unrealistic. Like Cindy, when the time came that April was no longer sheltered, she had proved herself spirited enough to change.

The circumstances of his sister's death were painful memories that Bolan knew were best left untouched.

But circumstances had spared April; in a way had made the already self-assured lady even tougher. On Mack's example, she had become a competent warrior.

Bolan thought back on the first bloody Monday of their love. The process of recall was like flipping through an album of photographs. He saw April naked, stripped of her clothes and her pacifism, holding off a sadistic mobster called Fuzz Martin with nothing but a steel spike. Bolan relived the relief he had felt when he found out she was still alive, and remembered the dark oath he had sworn against Fuzz Martin, that the mafioso would die horribly at Bolan's hands. Bolan's vivid memory remained faithful to his hatred for the one-time slimebucket, even though the guy was eventually offed by Harry "The Apeman" Venturi.

And since that first encounter with April Rose in Tennessee, a complete understanding had developed between Mack and April. The auburn-haired lady from the Agency no longer saw Striker as an immoral primitive, an uncivilized jungle-assassin doing evil work in a world where goodness could casually triumph. April had experienced the big man's war firsthand. She knew that Mack's difficult and ugly work was vitally important in a world where evil waited like a dormant virus, its attack attending the first signs of strain or apathy.

Although they rarely spoke of it, Mack also knew that April understood the place she occupied in his unusual life. The normal things could not be hers while her life was involved with Stony Man One. But Mack was confident that his free-spirited friend did not want "normal" things.

He slid the ridge of his index finger over the radio's dial as the night sky opened on a full moon past a bend in the hill-country road. He returned his hand to the wheel as Tammy Wynette's voice crooned, "Loneliness surrounds me, without your arms around me."

It always surprised Mack that he knew so little of April's past, despite the complete trust that existed between them. He could count the known details of her life before Stony Man on the fingers of his free hand. Fact: her father was a musician. Fact: her mother was a college instructor. Fact: she had once been engaged. Fact: before her on-campus recruitment she had been a peacenik with the Students for a Democratic Society—SDS—the moderate predecessor of the more radical Weatherman. Fact: long before Mack had met her she was an electronics, espionage and C3 expert of international quality. Hal had put it well when he once told Bolan, "She *is* the best."

Again, Bolan wondered why April had not responded personally to his recent phone call to Stony Man.

He knew there were dozens of routine tasks that could have occupied her at the precise moment of his incoming call.

Yet he also knew that there was no better tool for the warrior than intuition. Bolan had stayed alive many times by playing a hunch. He knew enough to trust himself now.

April had not answered the phone because something was wrong.

Bolan's mind switched to Hal Brognola. There were strange contradictions at work in Hal. The hard-nosed field agent, who now advised American presidents, hardly seemed a likely counterpart to the off-duty family man that Mack knew him to be. But he and the supercop faced a common enemy and The Executioner was proud that they both brought out the best in each other. So what was bugging Brognola in that phone call that couldn't wait for his return to Virginia?

Bolan was close enough to the rendezvous to ease up on the accelerator. He had made excellent time through the Pennsylvania night.

He could see the truck stop ahead where Hal would meet him at dawn.

The Executioner pulled off the road at a lookout. He killed the engine and the lights, and smoked a cigarette while his brain took in the cool night and its mysterious noises. The moon was down past the ridge, shedding a shower of silver light across half of Mack's vision. There was a breeze through the tops of the big pines. For now, it felt good to rest.

Here he could brood upon the essential loneliness of his life, and on how much he actually preferred it that way. When he had led his combat troops, Able Team and Phoenix Force, into forbidden waters off Cuba to attack the international KGB conspiracy at its most rabid, Bolan knew he was taking himself and his men beyond sanction, beyond the limits of all law, dooming each and every one of them to lives of endless danger from worldwide enemies. He knew, too, that his and his men's actions destined them to outright rejection by those who represented what was acceptable and respectable in society. Sure, it was lonely. But it was *real*. Their actions had made the stony men truly alive, despite the serious injuries sustained in that vicious encounter with Hydra.

As Bolan awaited the dawn in the Pennsylvania mountains, he felt the way he had felt during the lonely mission off Cuba. He felt like the falcon that ends up soaring over a cold ocean thousands of miles from the nearest land; with nowhere to light, it must keep winging through the crisp air forever.

Dawn rolled down the mountain in a gray mist that hung close to the piney tops.

Bolan swung himself upright from his cat-nap position behind the wheel and saw a Company car parked to one side of the truck stop. Hal was waiting for him.

The diner's chimney belched smoke into the fog. There were two tractor-trailer rigs in back, one running, the other with its cab curtains drawn. The diner itself was nestled in front of a curved stand of timber where the road dipped, came level, then climbed the side of the next hill. Reluctant to break the velvety quiet, Mack rolled down the empty mountain in neutral and brought his car parallel to Hal's.

BROGNOLA STOOD ACROSS THE ROOM facing the bar, with his back to Mack. Ordinarily he was no big drinker and Bolan tensed, wondering what made his friend look inside a bottle on this particular morning.

Hal must have felt Mack's eyes on the back of his head. He turned and said, "Let's talk in private."

They crossed the room without speaking and sat in a booth in the corner.

"This much you know already," Brognola began, his voice low but urgent. "The guy you've been scouring the Allegheny Mountains for is J.D. Dante. We needed photos of Dante to confirm his whereabouts and monitor his current activities, so you've been hunting him down where he was last seen. And I've been doing some hunting on my own. And I think we've both scored.''

''What's up?''

''My hunt was for rumor and gossip and information from interrogations. Let's start with that. I have established that our boy Dante has been tagged as meeting in the United States with Fyodor Zossimov, liaison with Moscow's international terrorism desk. Zossimov would only come here for a *specific* arrangement. He's a technical adviser. He firebombed a synagogue in Paris, blew up a bridge in Mexico City, shrapneled a school bus in Tel Aviv. Fyodor Zossimov deals out death.''

''I'll try to thank him in person,'' Bolan said.

''I hope you'll get the chance. Because right now we've got to find him.''

''Where's April?'' Bolan asked.

''April? I'm not in touch with her,'' Brognola said, his eyes glinting like chrome.

Bolan felt a twist in his stomach, like a muscle knotting. ''What do you mean, you're not in touch with her?''

''Let's take it from the top, okay? It'll be clearer that way.''

''I'm listening.''

Brognola nervously shifted his weight on the seat. ''Your own hunt has turned up a particular item. We do have a lead. A long shot, really.''

''This have to do with April?''

''Yes. Her idea.''

Bolan listened, his gaze stone cold.

"We analyzed the photos of the negs you sent back the first few days you were here in the Alleghenies. There were hundreds of faces to check."

"Yeah, I shot a lot of pictures. Things were going well till I came across that paranoid doper in Susqua. Probably sleeping it off somewhere this morning."

"Nope," Brognola sighed, shaking his head. "I just ran a check through the local sheriff. He went to this Grayson Strummer's cabin. Empty. Except for some bloodstains."

"Could have been from our fight."

"Too much blood."

Bolan frowned. "I don't get it."

"Me neither. And it gets worse."

"Tell me about it."

"Your surveillance pattern has been an extended loop, starting down around Lock Haven and moving northwest higher into the Alleghenies, then swinging back through Treetop, Pineridge, and Susqua. You took hundreds of candid shots of men fitting the vague description we've got of Dante. You even got some damn fine telephoto shots of the people on farms and living back in the woods. None of them turned out to be Dante."

"There'd better be a 'but' in here soon."

"But," Brognola nodded, "there was one face that we made. At least April did."

"Whose?"

"A man called Byron York."

"Wait a second. That's the guy—"

"Right. The guy Grayson Strummer wanted to take you to."

Bolan leaned across the table, his eyes ablaze. "What's going on, Hal? Who is this guy and what's April have to do with him?"

Brognola cleared his throat. "She knew him from college, Striker. Seems they were, uh, engaged for a short time, until Byron York went his way and April went hers. The romance ended abruptly. She was strong-willed even then, knew what she was about. Meantime, York drops out of sight, bums around campuses organizing rallies, then disappears altogether a few years ago. Until you snap this photo and April recognizes him."

Brognola produced an 8 x 10 recon print. Bolan had taken the picture with a telephoto lens, so it was somewhat grainy. It was a shot of ten or twelve men watering their horses at a stream just a few hundred yards down a hill where Bolan had been snapping shots of a farmhouse. Bolan had clicked off a few shots of the riders and went back to focusing in on the farmhouse.

Now he studied the proffered photo with a frown.

Byron York had a thick gunslinger's mustache, but otherwise he was clean-shaven. His hair was close-cropped, barely an inch long all around. His face looked hard. He looked like a man living with a great change within him, or with a great loss.

"Okay, Hal," Bolan said, looking up. "You've given me enough deep background. Now tell me where April is."

"She went after him. Byron York."

"You sent her out on a field assignment?"

"I didn't send her, she sent herself," Brognola said.

The waitress had materialized at their booth. "You boys aren't arguin' over a girl now, are you?" Bolan's hard face shifted from Brognola to a plump middle-aged woman with winged rhinestone glasses and a pink waitress cap. Her name tag declared her as Doris.

"No reason for you to fight over a woman, boys," she continued. "'Specially you, cutie," she said to Brognola. Doris's wink dissolved some of Hal Brognola's lethal mood. "I brought'cha coffee, boys, now I'll take your orders. You can have anythin' you want, long as it's the special."

"Ham and eggs, sunnyside," Brognola muttered.

"The same," Mack said.

"Well, now," intoned Doris, "two specials. Ain't that convenient." The two men smiled bleakly. Doris was obviously pleased. She leaned on the table in front of Hal and whispered, "What's long and hard, honey?" The Fed's jaw dropped. Doris laughed. "I don't know where your mind is, fella. I was talkin' 'bout third grade!"

Doris left them with a chuckle to fetch their orders. Hal's smile lingered for a moment, then he turned to Bolan and held up his right hand to prevent Mack from speaking. "Okay, okay. Here's the goods."

Bolan listened as Hal described how April recognized her former fiancé, the onetime SDS activist Byron York, friend to J.D. Dante. According to Hal, it made operational sense for April to go in pursuit of York.

"Makes sense, does it?" Bolan said, his eyes as friendly as a night in Siberia.

"Yeah, dammit, it does."

"But something's wrong. What?"

"We're expecting her to call," confessed Hal. "But it's just not happening."

"How long, Hal?"

Brognola recognized the arctic quality in the voice, from the old days when Bolan had treated him like any other inconvenient cop—a stranger at best, more likely an enemy. "How long?"

"In another three hours she'll have been out of contact for one day."

Bolan's eyes narrowed.

Brognola's attention shifted to a large man in work boots strutting toward their booth. The trucker was unable to see Mack. His eyes were fixed on Brognola.

The trucker rested his huge hands on the table in front of Hal and leaned into the Fed's face. The guy wore a nasty leer. Across the table Mack could smell the reek of chewing tobacco. He knew Hal was getting a face full of the stink. "These seats are for truckers only, son," the giant boomed. "My rig's the only one sittin' in the yard. So move."

It had taken until this moment for Mack Bolan

to realize the kind of stress Hal Brognola was under. He saw Hal's worry for April surface into anger on the Fed's face. He wondered how the trucker remained unimpressed. The outsized dumbo had just stepped into the crater of a seething volcano.

Bolan rested his left palm on the man's right hand and anchored it to the table. "We're busy, friend," he said, in what at first appeared to be a reasonable tone. The man turned to Bolan for the first time.

Bolan caught his eyes and waited for the true threat beneath his words to penetrate. The man's expression began to change. He realized he could not move his arm.

"Yer jest gonna have to stop socializin' and let these boys to their breakfast." It was Doris. Mack admired the way she inserted her body between the trucker and the table. She gave her hips a little gyration and pressed herself against the trucker. Mack released the hand and its owner left, muttering.

"Don't be bothered 'bout that one," Doris chattered at them. "He comes through here every week and causes a little stir every time. Never anythin' major, y'unnerstand—jest a fart in the overall thunderstorm." She set the platters before the two men and disappeared.

"Everyone around here is crazy," Hal reflected to no one in particular. "Look, Mack, I didn't tell you over the phone because we needed some info from Washington, which took a while to get. I didn't want you to be working blind."

"What was the problem?" Bolan asked.

"The ISA again. Not the boys themselves but some file clerk. He refused to release anything about Zossimov's recent appearance in the U.S., nor would he confirm new ideological trends in Dante's crowd, including York."

For Bolan, Brognola's statement summarized the dangers of waging a war that had become too impersonal. Yeah, Bolan had heard of the ISA. They were military—the Army's Intelligence Support Activity. They were first put together under the Carter administration to augment the efforts of both the CIA and DIA in collecting info for the ill-fated attempt to free the American hostages.

Most recently they had been running supersensitive missions against KGB-backed terrorists in the current political hotspots of Central America. Mack Bolan knew some of those men in Nicaragua and El Salvador. They were good men. But to Bolan's knowledge, even the best men in an impersonal war were hamstrung by the strange workings of bureaucracies.

This was not Stony Man's first foul-up involving the ISA. Weeks before, Mack Bolan had been bumped—bumped!—from an already guaranteed position in the intensive Russian immersion course at San Diego Naval Base. No satisfactory explanation had been given, but Hal Brognola had not been content to let it rest. Using his influence as presidential adviser, he had been able to pry into the military's internal affairs just enough to catch a rumor that ISA personnel had first dibs on the military's Russian courses, for now and for time to come.

Mack Bolan could not blame or hate the brave men of the ISA. But if April Rose was harmed as a result of this recent delay, he would pay a short visit to the file clerk.

"What did you get, Hal?" Bolan said carefully.

"Just the location of York's camp." Hal had a slight smile for this solitary bit of good news. "Oh, yeah," he continued, "I forgot to mention, I authorized a flyover. Those cameras on the C-103s sure can do miracles. Anyway, we've got a fix on April's jeep."

"In the camp?"

"Yeah, but no April outside and no Dante."

"Then this soft probe has just gone hard."

Brognola motioned for the bill, and Doris brought it fast. "Hope to see you boys back real soon," she said. Bolan saw there was a handwritten phone number on the chit that she handed to Hal. The Fed shot her a puzzled look, but Bolan noticed he left a big tip.

3

The sentry spun just in time to see the moonlight skate along the thin steel blade a second before it punctured his left eye.

His sawed-off Browning shotgun dropped from his hands as thick globs of blood squirted out into the night.

The dying man sank to his knees.

Bolan scampered up the incline and ducked behind a thick pine tree. He slapped the knife back into its sheath, engaged the Beretta 93-R's folding carbine stock plus modified sound suppressor and flash hider, and loaded the machine pistol with a 15-round box magazine.

His tight nightsuit blended him into the cool darkness.

This had not been a hasty operation, just a speedy one.

That morning, Brognola had punched a lot of phone numbers to keep a few expensive Washington computers humming, and finally he got what he was after: data about Byron York and what the man was doing in the backwoods of Pennsylvania.

The answer had confirmed all the worst suspicions.

York had abandoned his previous left-wing radicalism years ago, exchanging it for a far-right radicalism.

Instead of floating about the countercultural underground, he had become leader of a group of fanatical survivalists. Sixty-three of them, including some with families, had set up their own makeshift camp, where they lived as much as possible off the land and waited for the financial and/or military collapse of the United States.

Bolan watched from the shadows.

He saw that every man, woman and child walking around the camp carried a gun. At least half of them looked anxious to put their weapons to use.

The camp itself was well planned, nestled in a clearing surrounded by thousands of towering pine trees.

Within the clearing, a dozen or so log cabins were visible, constructed in a semicircle; another dozen were under construction to complete the circle. Those people not yet installed in cabins made do with tents of various sizes huddled within the circle.

Directly in the center of the camp was a large firepit, alive with a pulsating fire the size of a municipal water fountain. This was no ordinary survivalist camp. This was an extreme fringe, the furthest reach of a political passion, cold in its steely determination, and crazed in its extremity.

Bolan spotted the primer-painted new Hummer jeep that April had checked out of the Stony Man Farm's motor pool. The light from the campfire revealed the crowd of bullet holes that had chewed up the rear left fender and half of the driver's seat.

Bolan dropped to the ground. Within seconds the nightfighter was clawing across the dirt and dried pine needles, the 93-R cradled against his chest.

These people were about to receive their final exam in survival.

And most of them would fail.

4

"I think he's gonna kill her."

"Huh?"

"Kill her. Byron's gonna have to kill her."

The man made a quick slashing motion across his throat. He mouthed the word "kill."

The second man was wearing a Sony Walkman headset clamped over his Red Sox baseball cap. He nodded understanding and smiled. He had an M-16 slung over one shoulder and was peeling an orange in the darkness, dropping the peels on the ground as they walked.

Mack Bolan was crouched behind a thick bush, ten yards from April's bullet-riddled jeep. Unknowingly, they blocked his approach.

But not for long.

"I wouldn't throw them peels around, Jeff," the first man warned. "Byron'll have your ass."

"Huh?" Jeff said.

The first man grabbed one side of the headset and bent it away from Jeff's ear. "I said, Byron'll have your ass."

"No way," Jeff grinned. "Not as long as he's got hers." He leered toward the cabin behind them.

Bolan's muscles burned, hungry for movement.

The first man leaned his XM-10 semiautomatic against the jeep and pulled out a pack of Camels, shaking one out of the pack and sticking it in his mouth. He lit it, flicked the match into the dark. It trailed smoke like a comet. "Byron'll kill her for sure," he repeated, now that Jeff had removed the headset.

"I doubt it."

"He killed that big ox, didn't he? Grayman."

"Grayson. He didn't, that friend of his did. The weird dude with all the guns."

"Still, she saw us burying the chump's body, which makes her a witness. And the rest of us accessories to murder. She can finger us."

Jeff snorted, shoved a section of orange into his mouth. "You picked up a lot of law in prison, man."

"Enough to know she's gotta die. And if Byron don't wanna do it, some of us will. Gladly."

"Yeah," Jeff grinned. "I'd like to get it into her—"

Bolan sprang from the bush, the Beretta's stock wedged against his shoulder. The two men stared at the apparition with the camouflage smears striping his face. The first guy's cigarette dropped from his mouth and bounced down the front of his shirt.

Jeff recovered quicker and snatched up his M-16.

Bolan squeezed the trigger. The gun chuffed out half a dozen bullets through the soft fleshy hollow of Jeff's throat. Blood sprayed out in a sunburst, drenching flannel shirt and khaki pants as the corpse collapsed.

Jeff's partner caught Bolan's next missiles in a vertical row down his sternum, splitting open his chest like an orchid in bloom. The guy flipped backward into the jeep, banged his head on the fender, slid to the ground dead.

Thanks to the suppressor and the flash hider, no one came charging out of cabins or tents. A couple of men a hundred yards away walked by the campfire and threw a few logs on it; the giant fire crackled and snapped loudly as if it were chewing the wood instead of burning it. Bolan booted the two corpses to the side, rolling them into a clump of mountain laurel.

Then he crouchwalked to the cabin where the two dead guards had indicated April was being held.

The window shades were made of heavy burlap; nothing could be seen through them. He pressed his ear against the glass, heard an old song by Jefferson Airplane that his younger brother used to play about the time Mack first hit Nam. Beneath the pounding song he could barely make out the voices. One was April's.

Bolan took two deep breaths, gripped the Beretta, unleashed his muscles. So fluid were his movements they seemed to surpass light and become one with time. Fury was everything, everywhere.

His shoulder rammed into the thick wood. The deltoid and latissimus dorsi muscles were bunched like a fist. They smashed the door open with such force that it tore free from one of its hinges and dangled precariously.

The door barely slowed Bolan's pace. He charged through the tiny kitchen area, stacked with dirty dishes, and into the main cabin. He dived in a tuck-and-roll over a sofa and bumped up against the stone fireplace.

His eyes had already snapped half a dozen mental pictures of the room while in midflight, developing and processing them as he tumbled across the dusty wooden floor, studying them for targets as he swung the Beretta into place.

April was seated to his left in an old-fashioned rocking chair. The skin on her wrists was chafed raw by the rough rope binding them together; a blood-soaked bandage was wrapped awkwardly around her upper left arm. Ten feet to Bolan's right was a thin, weasely man with a scarred face. He was clutching an Uzi semiauto carbine to his skinny chest. Standing behind April was the square brooding face of Byron York. No apparent weapon. That made him a secondary target.

The scar-faced sentry hissed as he jabbed the Uzi's muzzle toward Bolan. The Beretta boiled out its hornets from hell. The Uzi tumbled to the floor. The dead man twisted around with a last groan and flopped into the table, knocking the cassette player to the floor. The corpse fell on top of it, muffling the insistent beat of Jefferson Airplane.

Bolan spun around toward Byron York. The guy remained motionless behind April's chair. Bolan's finger twitched anxiously at the trigger, but something stopped him from shredding York into blood-soaked confetti.

The mission.

Yeah, the mission.

"You never miss a beat, Mack," April Rose said. Her face glowed with relief.

"That's the way I stay alive. What's *your* secret, April?"

She was stung by his sarcasm, the sharp impatience of a man pushed too long and too hard, but she recovered fast.

"I never miss a beat, either," she said. "I got your number and it's my number, too. And I'm picking up on the way numbers fall."

Bolan waved the Beretta at York. "Back up three steps, guy. Move!"

York held his hands high as he obeyed the command.

Bolan slid the Fairbairon blade from its sheath and sawed through the rope wrapped around April's wrists.

April stood up. She rubbed some circulation back into her bruised wrists. Then she pried the Uzi SAC from under the dead sentry's body, wiped the blood off to avoid slip, and held the machine gun at hip level, poised and impressive.

But she was looking sheepishly at Bolan. "I guess I blew it, huh?"

Byron York stepped forward impatiently. "Just who is this guy, April?"

April turned to him and jabbed her Uzi into his stomach. "There's no time for explanations now, Byron. Just tell us where J.D. Dante is."

"So that's it," he said.

"That's it," Bolan said.

"Where is he?" April repeated.

"I don't know."

Bolan thrust the Beretta's metal jaws of death into York's face.

York flinched. "I don't *know*, man. Bastard waltzes in here a few days ago, wants me to hide him out until he can grab the caboose."

"The caboose?"

"Yeah. Radical Express. A sort of underground railroad to California. He had some business out on the West Coast and needed to stay out of sight for a couple of days."

"Why'd he come to you?" Bolan asked. "This group isn't sympathetic to the Weather Underground's cause."

"Nobody here knew who he really was. Just me. They figured he was a mercenary because of his guns."

April shook her head. "You got out of that madness, Byron. Why'd you help him?"

"Didn't have much choice. J.D. carries a grudge like a pocketknife. Sharpened and ready to use. He could nail me with the cops, too. I drove for him in a heist, back when I was with Weatherman. The cops could hassle me for years."

"What about Grayson Strummer?" Bolan asked.

"You wanna know about that poor son of a bitch?" Byron York said. "He'd been trying to join up with us for months. But I made a rule up here: no drugs. So we wouldn't take him. Then he tells one of my men that a stranger's been following him, snapping pictures. J.D. hears about it, takes a couple of my men and goes after Grayson to interrogate him. Grayson's just a dumb ox, but J.D. thinks he's holding out on him. Insists all that fancy photography equipment in Grayson's room belongs to him. Thinks he's a spy. So the three of them beat the slob to death. Now he's got me and my people involved in murder. Screw it all. Screw all of you." He ran an anxious hand through his short dark hair.

"We have to find him," Bolan said, flicking the tip of the machine pistol's barrel under York's chin. "Now."

"You'll be lucky to get out of this camp alive," smirked York. "And trying to find J.D. on the Radical Express—you'd be trying to grab smoke."

"That's why you're coming with us," Bolan told him. "You're gonna be our engineer."

York's face froze. "Call your dog off, April. For old times' sake."

"We're not talking old times, guy," Bolan

said. "We're talking new times. I'm changing every day, you know that? You have to haul ass to keep up with me." He shoved the barrel up under the survivalist zealot's clenched jaw. "I guess you came across me at the wrong time in my life. In one way or another, you will never recover from this, I can assure you. I am the choices you never made, punk, and they have come home to haunt you. Know anything about choices? You think you're so different from me?"

Bolan thrust the barrel upward once more. York spoke dryly, his neck at a tilt, his chin stuck in the air. "Choices are something I don't have. Apparently you do."

"No, you're not like me," Bolan decided, waving the gun toward the door. "April, the keys."

April snatched them up from the table next to the sofa.

"How's the Hummer running?" he asked.

"It's fine—the bullets didn't get anything vital, only the driver."

Bolan pointed the Beretta. "Let's go."

They moved out of the cabin into the crisp night air, crouching low in single-file formation. April went first, her finger taut against the Uzi trigger, her auburn hair whipping in the night breeze. York followed, weaponless, eyes darting nervously. Bolan covered them from behind, his Beretta relentlessly sweeping a wide arc as they ran.

Within seconds they were in the jeep. Bolan reached under the vehicle and dragged the XM-10 free from one of the dead guard's hands. He tossed it to York. The two men exchanged hard looks.

Bolan was taking a calculated risk, but York was taking his only chance. York's survivalist associates would blame him for what had happened. Bolan was right; real survival meant choice, making the right choice, the one that lets you survive. York knew what his choices were damn well. He realized there was something about this black-clad warrior that he shared. "Survival, then. Long term," he said. "Right now I'm with you."

Bolan balanced his Beretta across his lap and poked the key into the ignition. Next to him, April turned in the passenger seat, propping the Uzi on the back of her seat. Behind them, York hunkered down, his XM-10 pointing out the back.

"The only access road in or out is blocked by guards," York added. "I know because I posted them there."

"I know, too," Bolan said. The jeep roared to life with a violent shudder.

People poured suddenly from their cabins and tents, alerted by the noise, their shirts open and flapping, pants unbuckled, shoeless.

They all brandished guns.

The few curious women and children were shoved brusquely aside as the men ran toward the revving jeep. Bolan rammed the Hummer into gear, spun the machine around, jammed the gas pedal to the floor.

Dirt and pine needles swirled behind the spinning wheels as the vehicle bolted down the narrow dirt road and out of the open camp.

April and York kept up fire, spitting molten gutgrinders through the dark forest. Bolan saw two men crumple in the rearview mirror. A slug thudded dully into the metal frame of the jeep.

Bolan maneuvered down the dark tree-lined dirt road without headlights. Rocks, ruts and thick exposed roots kept the ride bumpy.

A sudden curve loomed and Bolan banked the jeep a little too sharply, bouncing the rear fender off a huge pine tree. April was tossed six inches into the air, the Uzi almost flying out of her hands. Bolan flicked on the headlights.

York called out to Bolan. "Within minutes we're gonna run into two surplus jeeps and four heavily armed greasers who've waited all their lives for an opportunity like this."

"Maybe," Bolan said.

"Ain't no maybe about it. SOP. This is the only road and they're at the bottom heading our way. I don't like the odds."

April smiled grimly. "He's beat the odds before, Byron."

"Well, I don't like it—"

A burst of semiautomatic fire flashed twenty yards in front of them, stitching a line across the hood. One of the headlights exploded, spraying glass into the air. It sprinkled onto their shoulders as Bolan jerked the wheel hard, tugging the jeep into a zigzag pattern while April leveled her Uzi ahead.

Another burst of fire from the other side of the road. The zigzagging jeep swept a single headlight through the woods. As a burst of fire came from ahead, the light washed over another enemy—on horseback. He was unshouldering an M-16.

"Take the guy on the horse," Bolan shouted. "I've got the other one."

The man ahead stood spread-legged in the middle of the road and fired another series into the car. Half of the windshield blew out of its metal frame.

Bolan aimed the jeep directly at the bastard and slammed the gear into fourth. The vehicle growled hungrily as it roared toward him.

The guy tried for the foot-high embankment on the side of the road, leaping aside and praying for a foothold.

Bolan bumped into the embankment. He kept the pedal down. The jeep devoured the sandy embankment, plowing forward and bulling into the scrambling gunman, flipping him up onto the jeep's bullet-scarred hood and rolling him into the shattered windshield, as if to give him an inventory of the damage he had done.

The body fell, and the back left wheel crunched over his chest, grinding sharp splinters of ribs through most major organs.

Meantime, April and York were pruning the forest with a dozen torpedos that sought the rider, not the horse. At least four of them found their mark, punching through a shoulder, a hand, the chest, finally the groin. The last bullet yanked the rider out of his saddle with a scream that terrified the horse. The roan reared back, trampling its rider's face into bloody mush before it galloped away, deep into the dark woods.

Bolan did not let up on the gas.

He had survived all these years by following a very simple philosophy: if you're already dead, it's harder to kill you. A warrior's philosophy, not often understood by civilians. It is as ancient as the *Hagakure* of Yamamoto Tsuetomo: "The way of the Samurai is found in death." It is as modern as a cop answering a call for a domestic squabble. Once you have accepted your own death and the inevitability of it—we all die, but few accept the fact—then you cannot be bullied or threatened. You are more complete as a warrior and a man. The dark side of human nature, the source of the drive to take life, unites with the side of nature that seeks only justice, that is guided by the light. The acceptance of mortality brings together a man's possibilities and helps him take aim with them. The criminal and the saint are, at their best, united in their acceptance of death. In death, Bolan would always be at his best: death was the condition of his life.

The echo of approaching cars came through the trees.

Bolan swerved the jeep off the road. He bounced between the trees.

"What the hell are you doing?" York demanded.

"Shut up, Byron," April snapped.

"He's heading us straight for the Allegheny River," York yelled in panic.

Bolan wove the jeep through the trees, bouncing off an occasional trunk like a pinball. They could hear the churning of the nearby river. Behind them they heard the whine of engines and the shouts of their pursuers. Closer and closer.

The woods became too thick to drive through. "This is where we get out," Bolan said. "We walk the rest of the way."

"I was afraid you'd say that," York grunted.

"Move it, York. They catch us, they'll go harder on you than us."

Bolan stopped, peered at the creases of pain lining York's face, saw his hand pressed against his right side. Then he saw the dark blood oozing between the fingers. "How bad you hit?"

"Bad enough."

The rumble of engines grew louder. Angry voices.

York choked out a laugh; it sent him into a coughing spasm. "This is the scene where I hold 'em off while you two get away, right? I think I've seen this scene before."

Bolan tucked his Beretta into its holster. Then he lifted York out of the jeep.

They jogged off through the woods, Bolan leading the way with York slung across his shoulders in a fireman's carry. April followed, glancing over her shoulder to watch for those who hunted them.

The ground began sloping. Through the thinning trees a rock-strewn shore became visible. The mighty Allegheny. The river bubbled here and there, its current swift but not treacherous. The moon spilled light across it like the pale underbelly of a giant fish.

Bolan could tell from the limp weight that York had passed out. The wound must have been worse than York had indicated. Bolan needed him alive. He was their only link to the Radical Express. He was to be their "engineer," the man who got them aboard. Only York knew where they could get aboard and who the "station-masters" were.

A shotgun blast brought in a swarm of pellets that sparked across the rocks where Bolan and April ran. April pivoted, squeezed a burst of her own, heard a cry of pain, turned to concentrate on keeping up with Bolan. He was running through the water now, splashing by the side of a high embankment with no sloping shore.

"What now?" she gasped as she ran, the water soon waist deep. Then she saw it.

Tucked flush against the embankment was a small motorboat, anchored under some camouflage brush. Bolan laid York gently in the middle of the boat, hoisted himself over the side, then balanced the craft while April climbed in.

Bolan yanked on the starter and the motor sputtered to life. A quick slash at the anchor rope and they were skimming across the top of the river, heading downstream toward Bolan's automobile. The boat was dragging slightly. Bolan had not counted on the weight of a third passenger.

The hunters were rushing through the brush, firing blindly as they ran down toward the shore. Bullets splashed in the water. April returned fire, her Uzi snarling like a hound.

The nearest man behind them had waded into the water and was firing both barrels of his shotgun when April drilled a burst of bonemashers at him. He flopped backward in the water. Part of his face floated downstream. The rest of him sank.

Bolan held the rudder with one hand and fired the Beretta with the other. Two 9mm spikes hammered into an enemy skull, sending the back of it spinning into the night like a hairy Frisbee.

Bolan guided the boat around a bend as the river twisted into a severe S. Finally they were out of range.

"We're moving away from the path," Bolan muttered. "They can't follow us."

April slumped in exhaustion. Then she wedged the Uzi into the bow. Automatically she turned to tend to Byron York.

"There's a hospital twelve miles south of here," Bolan told her.

April tugged at York's closed eyelids, pressed her fingertips against his neck. Her voice quavered when she looked up.

"Too late, Mack. He's dead."

Their eyes locked.

"He was a lousy survivalist," Mack said. "He got it all wrong." He looked at the dim outline of the dead man. "There's the proof."

5

"Hey, lady." The old black man waved at April. "How 'bout a nice tattoo?"

April smiled, shook her head.

"Nothin' big, mama. A rose on your thigh. You'll see, drive your man wild."

"Some other time maybe," April said.

The old man shrugged good-naturedly and bent over the customer he was working on. The compact machine in his hand buzzed angrily as the sharp inking needle bobbed up and down like a sewing machine. The elaborate blue wings of a dragon began to appear on the customer's skin.

"See anything you like?" Bolan said. He had appeared suddenly at her side.

"He wants me to get a rose on my thigh. Says it'll drive you crazy."

Bolan grinned. "It would."

"You sure this is the right place?" April said nervously.

"Right upstairs there. Goodey's Gym. I ran a quick recon on the place. There's a fire escape from the second floor, just in case we need to make a quick scram. Ready?"

April took a deep breath, nodded. "Let's do it."

They started up the stairs.

It was less than twelve hours and half a dozen bodies since they had blasted their way out of the survivalist village. For all they knew, the late Byron York was still floating around on the Allegheny River in the motorboat.

There had been a moment's hesitation as they hopped out of the boat and splashed their way to shore. April had paused, glanced over her shoulder at Byron York's lifeless body. The left arm dangled over the side, the fingers grazed the water like those of a lazy fisherman enjoying the solitude. She had spun sharply then and climbed toward the car, never looking back. They rocketed out of there, tires screaming through the sleepy woods until they found a public telephone.

Hal Brognola had listened to everything without interruption, letting Bolan finish every detail over the scrambled wire.

"Can you keep them off our backs for a while?" Bolan had asked.

"No sweat. Local law enforcement will have them rounded up in no time. Most of them will be behind bars for the murder of Grayson Strummer. The rest we'll keep occupied." A slight pause indicated that Hal was puffing thoughtfully on his cigar. "The way I read the situation now, York is dead, therefore the mission is dead. No way to trace Dante—we'll have to wait until he surfaces."

"Maybe not," Bolan said.

"Oh?"

"There's another possibility."

"Spill, Striker. What haven't you told me?"

"April overheard a name. We don't know what it means exactly, but she thinks it's a stationmaster."

"Stationmaster?"

"Yeah. A guy who puts people on the Radical Express, the 'underground railroad' system that stretches from Florida up to Canada, and from New York across to Los Angeles, with a few side tracks to Mexico, Cuba, Hawaii. It's a wilderness route more often than not, cutting through tracts that never see a cop, never see people. It's going to be tough."

"What's the name?"

"Newton. 'Gravity' Newton."

"Gravity Newton? That some kind of joke?"

"It's his fight name. He's a boxer. April heard Dante and York talking about him. Dante said something like, 'I hope Gravity's found an easier way to check out passengers.'"

"You have a location for this Gravity Newton?"

"Nope. If I did your job, Hal, what would be left for you write about in your memoirs?"

Brognola laughed. "Give me your number." Bolan did. "Wait there."

Brognola hung up.

Five minutes later the pay phone jangled through the dark Sunoco station. A distant night bird tried to imitate the sounds as Bolan snatched the receiver. "Yeah?"

"Wilkes-Barre. Goodey's Gym."

"Got it. Anything else?"

There was a pause. Silent telephone wire stretched across three states. Then, "See you in California, Striker."

Click.

THE SIGN ON THE PEELING WALL was handmade, hastily scrawled with a black felt marker on the back of a cardboard flap torn from a packing box.

Goodey's Gym. Second Floor.

A faded gray arrow pointed up the stairs for those too punch-drunk to realize where the second floor might be. Above the cardboard sign was a fancy handcarved wooden sign with painted flowers, a Christian cross, a Star of David and a plump grinning Buddha.

"Covering all their bets," April said, pointing at the sign.

Church of Universal Being. Second Floor. Through Gymnasium.

They climbed three steps. On the wall was a jagged white line about a foot long, scratched through the paint with a knife. Written above the line in pen was the caption: Floodline. June 20, 1972. Thanks, Agnes.

"What's that mean?" April asked.

"Tropical storm Agnes came through here that year and wiped out a lot of the Eastern Seaboard.

Killed a hundred twenty-nine people, left another hundred fifteen thousand homeless. Damage added up to more than three billion dollars.''

"I remember that now. I was eighteen. My sophomore year. Those newspaper photos of houses floating through shopping malls. People rescued from their attics by boat. It was horrible."

"Yeah, Wilkes-Barre was mostly underwater. It's taken this long for a lot of people to get back on their feet again. Those that could."

As they climbed the narrow stairs, they heard the sounds of heavy punching bags being whomped, speed bags being pummeled rhythmically, felt the vibration of men running in place. The odor was strong and slightly sour. The smell of heavy sweat. And something more. Desperation. Hope. Anger. Exhaustion.

Bolan squeezed April's arm. "Let's get the show on the road. Remember, act sexy."

The place at the top of the warped stairs was obviously Goodey's Gym. The huffing and panting of activity was everywhere. Fourteen boys and men jabbed, stalked, hooked and punched various bags and each other.

As they walked through the gym, Bolan noticed the break in concentration as the fighters caught sight of April. Gone were her wet jeans and sopping turtleneck sweater from last night. But even a hastily purchased denim skirt and plaid blouse from a cheap five-and-dime looked elegant on her. Bolan knew she had put herself through college as a professional model. She had a tall athletic body that had been honed on the swim team in high school. She still worked out regularly: aerobics, gymnastics, ballet. That was one of the things that separated her from those who starved themselves to thinness, and who had no tone to their muscles. April's body looked capable, useful.

"You lost, sport?" asked a fat bald man in a dirty white shirt. Sweat stains wreathed his armpits. He scratched his swollen gut as he spoke, looking April up and down with glazed eyes.

"Who runs this place?" Bolan asked.

The fat man jerked his head to the right. "Frank Goodey. The guy with the cucumber nose behind the counter there." He studied Bolan for a moment with darting, appraising eyes. "You a fighter?"

"When I have to be."

"Southpaw?"

"Sometimes."

"Kind of old for the game, aren't you?"

"Kind of fat to be asking personal questions, aren't you?"

"Hey, man," growled a big kid about seventeen, stepping away from the heavy bag he'd been hitting. "Watch your mouth, pal. That's my manager you're wisin' off to."

Bolan had not moved his eyes from the fat man, who winced from the glare, turned and shoved his fighter back toward the bag. "Just keep jabbing, kid. Quit dropping the right.

How many times I gotta tell you that? Jab, jab, jab!''

Bolan and April walked over to the window counter. The small room on the other side was filled with a thick haze of cigarette smoke. All of it came from the thin man with the cucumber nose.

''You Goodey?'' Bolan asked.

The guy took a long drag on his cigarette without looking up from his paper, the *Racing Form*. Excess smoke curled out between his lips.

''I'm looking for Gravity Newton.''

This earned a heavy-lidded stare. Goodey screwed the cigarette into the corner of his mouth. As he dropped the paper onto his desk, ashes flew from the overflowing ashtray. His nose was flared and flat. An ex-pug's nose. ''Ten bucks.''

Bolan slid the bill across the counter top.

Goodey did not reach for it. Instead he grabbed a pair of sixteen-ounce Las-Dos boxing gloves and a set of Everlast wraps and tossed them onto the counter.

Bolan realized that the ten dollars was not for information but for equipment rental. ''I'm just here to talk,'' Bolan said.

''That's up to Newton. But people come to my gym to fight, not talk. I still got rent to pay.''

Bolan picked up the gloves and wraps. ''Where's Gravity?''

Goodey puffed out a cloud of gray smoke and nodded at the ring. Two boys barely in their teens were sparring, taking instruction from a muscular

Hispanic hanging on the ropes. "Newton's the one coaching."

"Thanks." Bolan tucked the gloves under his arm as he steered April by the elbow toward the ring. It was a raised platform that dominated half of the room.

"I guess this is the best approach," April sighed as her heels clattered across the wooden floor.

"Right now it's the only approach," Bolan muttered. "It's the only one we have time for."

Bolan guided April to one of the folding chairs ringside. She sat and crossed her legs. She revealed as much thigh as would cause enough distraction for Bolan to approach Gravity Newton.

"You Newton?" Bolan asked.

"Jab, Pablo!" the Hispanic urged, ignoring Bolan. "Don't slap. *Snap* it out." He turned, glanced down at Bolan with a frown. His face was young, early twenties, and still unmarked except for a slight scar under the left eyebrow. "I don't know you," he said and turned away. "Pick it away, Tommy. One quick movement!"

Bolan stepped up onto the platform. He leaned on the ropes next to Newton. The two men were about the same height and build. "I'm interested in doing some traveling. Friend of mine said you might recommend a safe method of transportation. Byron York."

Newton turned, looked Bolan up and down, then nodded at the gloves. "Put 'em on."

"These? Look, pal, I'm just here to talk about a mutual friend."

Gravity Newton smiled a perfect set of teeth and climbed between the ropes into the ring. "This is where I do all my talking."

Bolan had expected a test, but not this. He climbed down from the apron of the ring and walked over to April. "He wants to fight."

"Fight? What for?"

"Somebody desperate enough to get on the Radical Express obviously has to take a beating for the privilege," Bolan answered sourly. He peeled his shirt off and began winding the Everlast wraps around his hands, tying them off at the wrists. Then he slipped his hands into the spongy red gloves. "Tie them tight," he told April.

Newton had already herded the kids out of the ring and was stripped down to his trunks. He was bouncing up and down, smacking his gloved fists together. A plastic mouthpiece stretched his upper lip into a grotesque smile.

A few of the other fighters began to stare at the ring. A couple drifted over to watch, toweling sweat from their faces. Others followed.

"He looks hard," April whispered.

Bolan looked over his shoulder at Newton. "Yeah."

She squeezed the knot on the glove to make sure it was tight, then squeezed his hands through the padded gloves. "Good luck."

He nodded at her, turned and climbed up onto the ring. With a graceful movement he ducked between the ropes and began bouncing in his corner, loosening his legs and shaking out his arms. It wasn't the first time he had been in the ring. But the last time had been years ago, for fun. Since then, all the sport had gone out of his fighting. The purpose was no longer to win, it was to survive.

"Okay, *señor*," Gravity Newton called across the ring in his thick Hispanic accent. "When the bell sounds, we meet in the middle."

"How many rounds?" Bolan asked.

Newton laughed. "However many it takes."

6

The two hard men faced each other across the smooth canvas of the ring, the air between them thick with violence.

Bolan took deep breaths. One of the biggest problems boxers had in the ring was remembering to breathe correctly. Often they would charge ahead, throwing punches, blocking others; within minutes they'd be exhausted, because they had been breathing only sporadically, or shallowly, or not at all.

Bolan wore chinos and Nike sneakers. April carried the Beretta 93-R in her tote bag, since to these radicals it would be appropriate for two people on the run to have at least one gun. If neither of them had one, it would be suspicious.

The bell clanged starkly. The two men stalked toward each other. Bolan, stripped to the waist, displayed firm muscles, hard from constant use, forged in the furnace of deadly action daily, glistening now like marble.

Gravity Newton looked no less formidable. He was younger, perhaps, and with fewer scars. His dark skin was a map of the same bulging muscles that wrapped Bolan's body with taut grace, his stomach just as corrugated. The boxer tucked his chin down and bounced toward his amateur opponent.

Bolan easily picked off Newton's first jab. The second and third jabs were faster, but Bolan sidestepped them. He never even saw the fourth. It caught him on top of the forehead and sent him stumbling back several steps. A murmur arose from the spectators.

"You are fast, *señor*," Newton grinned. "But not fast enou—"

Bolan had feigned a movement to the right, now exploded a left hook over the top of Newton's rising left hand. It caught the young boxer on the ear. The guy's legs buckled slightly.

Before Bolan could follow up, Newton had danced nimbly out of the way.

Bolan chased him across the ring, hoping to tie him up, but he was no match for Newton's faster footwork. Bolan was already breathless from his natural response to attack and defense. It was nonstop and it was exhausting. Bolan knew there was no way he would beat a professional boxer in the long run. A punch in the face from a professional was the equivalent of being struck by a portable typewriter swung twice around the body.

Newton backed up against the ropes as Bolan pursued him, brought his gloves up to protect his face, pressed his elbows to his ribs to protect his body. Bolan snapped off a couple of jabs at Newton's face, but could not punch through the gloves. Then he ducked down and pummeled the body with two rib crackers, yet each was blocked by Newton's elbows.

He knew what Newton was doing, waiting to see if Bolan would punch himself out early, like most newcomers to the ring did. Anxious to win, or fearing to lose, they threw everything within the first minute of the round; then breathless and arm weary, they would be picked apart by their still-fresh opponent.

Realizing he was not going to break through Newton's defense, Bolan backed up into the middle of the ring and waited. Newton peered at him between his gloves.

Suddenly Newton was all movement, bobbing and weaving, dancing to the left and right—cutting the ring off, backing Bolan into the corner with zinging jabs and overhand rights.

Bolan managed to block many of the blows, knowing full well that Newton was not using all his speed or skill in this test. But a few bombshells managed to blast through.

A left hook twisted Bolan's head around; a body shot bruised his ribs. He felt the rope biting into his back as Newton pressed even closer, exhaling air through his flaring nostrils with each punch like a snorting dragon.

Bolan could have stayed in the corner until the end of the round, blocking most punches, surviving those he didn't. It might have been enough to pass this test of Newton's. No real physical harm would be done, a few bruises, some tender spots.

But that was not enough. Bolan needed some negotiating leverage with this "stationmaster."

He tucked his chin down, blocked Newton's hook and lurched forward. He thrust his fist into the Hispanic stomach. The fist hesitated when it slammed into granite stomach muscles, but Bolan rammed it into them again. And again. Until he felt Newton's body begin to sag from the blows.

Newton tried to punch his way out, but Bolan stayed right up against him, steam-drilling his punches to the body, never once letting Newton get his feet set. It was a clumsy maneuver, but it worked. It killed precious seconds and it kept the younger man from exhibiting any more boxing skills at the expense of Bolan's chin.

The Hispanic tried to push Bolan back. Bolan used his old football skills to keep burrowing in, pinning Newton against the ropes. He windmilled more punches to the body, largely just to keep Newton busy while the clock ticked closer to the end of the round. He figured there couldn't be more than twenty seconds left.

A lot could happen in twenty seconds.

Newton suddenly spun out of Bolan's grasp, double-pumping a torpedoing jab into Bolan's face. Bolan felt the non-sensation of his jaw going numb. A right cross hurtled at him like a truck. He barely managed to block it. But not so the follow-up left hook, which sledged him in the neck. He felt the vertebrae in his spine shift. Bolan was tired, real tired. Newton was circling him, flicking the left endlessly into his face.

Bolan covered up and bulled forward again, crowding Newton's long arms.

Taking advantage of no referee, Bolan kept Newton's arms trapped while he catapulted a sudden powerful uppercut that snapped Newton's mouth shut with a loud crack, lifting him slightly off the canvas and sending him reeling backward into the ropes.

Newton bounced off them from their tautness. He shook his head, then scowled at Bolan. He realized to what extent he had seriously underestimated his opponent's ability. He intended his expression to indicate that Bolan would be treated like a pro from now on. Mercilessly.

Newton bounced up on his toes. He brought up his gloves to the classic no-nonsense boxing stance and glided forward. It was unsettling to see a man recover so quickly from a punch as devastating as the one he'd just taken. Bolan had seen bigger men flop unconscious to the ground from a lesser blow. But boxers were not ordinary men. They were among the best conditioned athletes in the world. And this one was mad as hell.

The bell clanged for the end of the round.

Newton hesitated, obviously considered continuing the fight. Bolan waited with his fists raised, legs apart.

"First one you ain't decked within a minute," called a nearby pug good-naturedly. "Losin' yer touch, Gravity?"

The men continued to make jokes and laugh as they wandered away from the ring and back to their respective workouts. Within seconds the same old sounds of punching bags and rope skipping filled the gym as if nothing had happened.

Bolan climbed down from the ring and offered his gloves palm up to April. She began untying the laces.

His chest heaved as he gulped air. His face and body felt as if tenderized by a sledge hammer. On the other side of the room, Newton did not even look tired

"You okay?" April asked, trying to keep as calm as she could.

"Sure, sure. I murdered the bum."

"You kept him from murdering you."

"Same thing," Bolan smiled. He pulled off the gloves and unwound the wraps, his back purposely toward Newton. "What's he doing now?"

"Coming this way," she whispered.

Bolan did not turn around. He pretended not to notice Newton's approaching footfalls. When Newton was finally standing right next to him, Bolan looked up from the saturated wraps he was rolling.

"We talk now, *señor*," Newton said, and walked away.

Bolan and April followed him. April snatched Bolan's shirt from the chair and tossed it to him as they walked.

They marched briskly behind Newton. He strode to the far corner of the gym. Some old pieces of carpeting and torn punching bags were heaped in a pile. No one else was within listening range there.

A row of grimy windows lined the back wall, each so dirty that the sunlight was just a white blur, like a snowy TV screen. Wedged into one of the windows was a battered portable Zenith air conditioner, too small to do any good in a room that size. Newton flicked on the switch and the machine rattled to life, vibrating so much the glass in the window threatened to break.

"Goodey rents out the room in the back to the Church of Universal Being," Newton explained. "They missed a month's rent and he took their air conditioner from them. It's of no use to him, of course, but one appreciates the principle of the thing."

"And it will make it harder for anyone to overhear our conversation," Bolan said.

Newton shrugged. "Silver linings, my friend."

"Byron York sent us," April said. "We know him from—"

Newton held up his hands. "I do not want to know."

"But will you help us?"

"Yes."

"Just like that?" Bolan asked.

"Yes, just like that. You look unsure."

"Let's just say wary."

"I understand. So much in this world is not what it seems. People are not who they pretend to be. You might not believe that I was once a priest."

April looked shocked, despite her reserve and her silence.

"Yes. In my country, El Salvador. For years the clergy have been persecuted, bullied, threatened for talking out against the injustices of the Duarte government, and later Borjo. In 1981, thirteen thousand civilians were killed. The horrible became the unspeakable. An American priest managed to smuggle me out into your country. But when he went back to help others, they killed him, too." He paused, looked at the dirty windows. "His name was Father Frank Newton. I adopted his last name out of respect."

"You're an excellent boxer," April said.

"I am a fighter. I was always a fighter. I fought both the unholy government and the Communist invaders. El Salvador is for its people, not for bankers *or* Communists."

"Between a rock and a hard place," Bolan nodded. "I guess you weren't very popular down there, guy."

"Only with the people." Newton shrugged off the memory and smiled in resignation. "Here I fight in the ring and train young ones, keeping them away from the temptations of the street as best I can."

Bolan looked him in the eyes. "And your work as a stationmaster?"

"That, too, is my duty. My duty to those who wish to speak against their government freely, no matter what they have to say. That is why I do not want to know about your past, present, or future.

I do not care what you believe, only that you have the freedom to say it. I have nothing against this government. The United States has been good to me. I know that even a country like this can decay into one like mine unless the freedom to disagree is sacred. I do here what Father Newton tried to do in my country. And I must take the same risks he did."

"You are a strong man," April said.

Newton smiled. "So is your friend here. He's brave for getting in the ring. Most men refuse. They I do not help, for they lack the courage of their beliefs. Your need must be great."

"It is," Bolan said.

They began walking toward the exit.

"Where'd you get the name 'Gravity'?" April asked.

"Something for the media to remember me by. Goodey's idea. He tells them, 'Newton helps his opponents discover gravity.'"

Bolan rubbed his jaw. "I know what he means."

Newton reached into the pocket of his sweat pants and handed Bolan a folded sheet of paper. "This is the information you seek."

Bolan slipped it into his pocket without opening it. "Thanks."

"Have a safe trip."

"We hope so. We're trying to meet up with our friend, J.D. Dante."

Newton spun and stared at Bolan with barely concealed horror. "He is your friend?"

"Yeah. Can you tell us where we can catch up with him?"

"I do not want to doubt your words, but it is difficult for me to believe you are friends with this man Dante."

"Politics makes strange bedfellows," April explained.

"Apparently. For you do not seem to be washed in the same blood as he. I cannot tell you anything he may have told me. I never reveal another's words. They are like confession to me. But I will leave you with this warning. Be careful of your friend. He has the fever. He burns to kill."

"We'll remember," Bolan promised.

7

"You here for the series?" she asked.

Bolan turned around, still holding the blue Voit swim fins. "Excuse me?"

"The World Series. Most of my customers are regulars, but since I haven't seen the two of you before, I thought you might be here for the series. The town's always flooded with fans this time of year."

"Yeah, but the World Series...?"

"Oh, no, no. Not *the* World Series," the young redhead laughed. "The Little League World Series. Williamsport, Pennsylvania. Home of the Little League World Series. It's our only claim to fame."

"Right," Bolan nodded. "I remember now."

She brushed a bright strand of hair from her face and smiled. A galaxy of freckles splashed across her nose and cheeks, enhancing her already lovely face. She stood in tight khaki shorts and a blue T-shirt that advertised the shop they were standing in: Davey Jones's Diving Locker. The shirt was two sizes too small for her.

Bolan and April browsed through the diving shop, checking out the Conshelf 20 regulars and

Osprey masks. April moved to the other side of
the store. She read the label on a Seafarer wet suit.
A young man with a wispy blond beard was ring-
ing up a sale behind the other counter, bagging a
pair of Speedo swimming goggles for a teenaged
girl. There were no other customers in the store,
nor any other salespeople.

"You've got a lot of nice diving equipment,"
Bolan said to the girl in the T-shirt. "I wouldn't
think there'd be many places to dive around
here."

"There's the Susquehanna River and a bunch of
lakes scattered around. But most local divers
belong to the Nautilus Club."

"Nautilus?"

"Yeah, like those exercise machines, only we've
been around much longer than them. Everybody
thinks we're a weight-lifting group."

"Does the club take diving trips around the
country, like to California?"

"Sometimes. To the Bahamas, too."

"Have any trips to California coming up
soon?"

"Maybe. Why do you ask?"

"I may want to join your club. Me and my
friend." He nodded toward April.

The redhead looked confused. "I don't understand. You don't live around here, do you?"

"Nope."

"But you want to join our diving club?"

"Temporary membership. Good for one trip.
To California."

"Why not just fly out alone?"

"We like crowds."

She shrugged. "Well, if you're serious, I can ask the boss. But it'll probably cost you more with the club, considering dues and stuff."

"We're serious," Bolan said, staring into her eyes. "And we'll pay."

She seemed to flush slightly under his gaze, then turned away. "I'll ask." She brushed aside a decorative fishing net that draped a doorway behind her, and she disappeared.

April came to Bolan's side. "What's up?"

"I made contact, I think."

"This is the station?"

"Could be. It's a good front, a diving club. People tend to notice the equipment, not the faces."

The phone by the cash register buzzed. The skinny boy with the wispy beard stopped arranging the Sea Hawk diving knives long enough to answer it. "Hello?... Okay." He hung up and looked at Bolan and April with a bored expression. "You the couple interested in the Nautilus Club?"

"Yeah."

"You got a credit card?"

"Cash," Bolan answered.

"Let's go." The kid slipped around the fishing net and was gone.

Bolan and April followed the blond boy through the doorway. On the other side were rows of industrial shelves stacked with diving supplies.

The youth made a quick right turn around a shelf lined with black Aqua Lung air tanks. Bolan and April took the same turn seconds later.

April gasped out loud as she and Bolan made a sudden stop.

Standing in front of them was the redheaded salesgirl, the blond kid and a tall black man.

They were all pointing spear guns.

At April and Bolan.

"One twitch," the redhead said, "and you're dead."

8

Larry "The Bleeder" Strohman carried the telephone through the kitchen and across the concrete patio to the edge of the pool. "Here's the phone you wanted, J.D."

In the middle of the swimming pool, cradled in a floating deck chair, lounged J.D. Dante. A white sun visor was pulled low over his forehead and a too-sweet banana daiquiri was clutched in his right hand. In his left hand he pinched a half-smoked joint. He sucked a deep drag on the joint, held it for a few seconds, them grimaced as he let the smoke out of his mouth. "Where'd you get this shit, Bleeder?" he asked, flipping the joint into the pool. "Your dog get diarrhea and you decided to dry it out and smoke it?"

Bleeder shook his head vigorously. "N-no, J.D. It's local stuff. Guy I know rents a couple acres in the middle of some farmer's corn field."

"Corn field?" Dante laughed cruelly. "I'm smoking a *corn field*? You're pathetic, Bleeder." Dante drained the rest of his banana daiquiri, then tossed the glass over his shoulder. It splashed into the water and sank. He shifted the Colt .45 M-1911 that rested on his chest, scratched his pale skin, idly shifted the gun back again. J.D. Dante was never without a weapon, usually three or four. He never ate, slept, went to the toilet, or made love without a weapon touching his body. Most who knew him suspected it was as much a personal preference as a necessity.

"Well, don't just stand there, Bleeder. Bring the phone to me."

Bleeder tugged the extra-long phone cord so it snaked across the patio. He walked around to the other side of the pool and reached the phone over the edge to Dante. Dante lifted up a lazy hand, but the phone was still several feet away. He snapped his fingers with annoyance. "C'mon, c'mon, fool, give it to me."

"I can't reach you, J.D.," Bleeder said. "You'll have to paddle over here."

Dante lifted his head. His eyes were blazing with anger. "I don't have to do anything, pig. I told you what I want, *now do it*!" Dante snatched up his .45 and pointed it at Bleeder's crotch. "Do it, worm."

Bleeder walked around to the shallow end of the pool to the steps. He kicked off his imported Bally shoes and started walking into the pool, ignoring his expensive slacks and tailored shirt. He was used to this treatment. As a student at Columbia fifteen years earlier, he'd gotten his nickname because he came away bleeding from every student protest. Not because he had been clubbed by the cops like the others, but because his nose always started bleeding when he got excited. He became a joke among the radicals he hung out with, something of a mascot. But at least they let him hang around. They manipulated him, used his considerable inheritance to pay for signs, T-shirts, leaflets. But he knew it and it didn't bother him. He felt he belonged.

As Bleeder sloshed through the waist-deep water, he held the telephone over his head, keeping the phone cord taut, afraid that if it touched the water he might be electrocuted.

"Don't look so scared, Bleeder," Dante laughed. "There's not enough electricity in there to hurt you."

"Sure, J.D.," Bleeder said nervously, "I know that."

"Give it here." Dante yanked the phone from him and began punching in a secret number that only he and one other person knew. It rang twice before being answered.

"Yes?" a foreign accented voice said.

"It's me," Dante announced. "The line clear?"

"Yes. But we would be wise to maintain some elementary precautions."

"Your fancy lingo doesn't impress me, Zossimov. I know what I'm doing."

"Of course you do," Zossimov replied, his voice conciliatory. "If I did not believe that, we would not be working together."

"Don't jive me, pal. We're working together because we each get something from this horror show. You get some nifty publicity about the decadent West and social unrest that you'll milk in

Pravda. And the Weather Underground comes into its own as a political power again. Only this time greater than ever.''

"I admire your confidence, my friend.''

"Confidence, shit! I just know what I'm doing. Everything in this business is timing. The economy's in the toilet, unemployment is terrible and getting worse, we're playing games with South America like we did in Vietnam, and our relations with your country make it seem like we'll be nuked any day now. This is the time for my group to rise again. What goes around, comes around, Zossimov.''

"Perhaps. In any event, I have procured the necessary supplies as per our previous discussion. Everything will be installed before your arrival in California. Do you have your itinerary set?''

"So far. I'm hitting some of the major stations, whipping up some enthusiasm along the way. I want my people frothing by the time this thing goes down. Because what happens Sunday is only the beginning. After that day, the Weather Underground will pull a major revolutionary attack once a week. The bombs have already been built, the targets chosen. Public buildings mostly. Courthouses, police stations, schools—''

"Schools?'' Zossimov interrupted.

"Yeah, schools. It's time the smug Ozzies and Harriets of this country had the revolution brought into their homes. Time they saw some blood while it's still fresh.''

"Efficient philosophy, indeed.''

"Yeah, you people should know." Dante felt his own pulse pounding, his voice rising in excitement. He made an effort to calm himself. It would not do for Zossimov to think him out of control. "So what kind of figures did you people come up with?"

"Calculating the expected number of people gathered to be about four hundred thousand, combined with the strategic locations of the explosives and other items you mentioned—at least ten thousand injuries."

"Good. Maimed and crippled people are constant reminders. I want injuries, not casualties."

"My compliments to your planning. Very impressive."

"You bet your ass, man. I've been planning it for years. And two days from now it begins. If you think those Iranians had this country by the balls, wait until you see some of the things I've got planned."

"First things first, my friend," Zossimov reminded him. "And first we start with Sunday."

"Right. See you in two days." Dante hung up the phone and handed it back to Bleeder, who waited in the pool in drenched clothes. "That Ruskie's a bigger asshole than you are, Bleeder."

"I don't understand," Bleeder said. "I thought we were working with him."

"We're working for ourselves, guy. Remember that."

Bleeder turned and waded out of the pool. He

could feel the blood starting to trickle down the inside of his nose. A bad sign.

FYODOR ZOSSIMOV HELD DOWN THE PLUNGER on the phone for a few seconds, listened for the dial tone, then punched in a number.

He could hear the electronic chorus as elaborate coding systems kicked in, scrambling transmissions and receptions. He adjusted the portable digital scrambling device attached to his phone.

Finally the connection was completed and a surly voice said only one word. "Speak."

"Zossimov here. I have made contact."

"And?"

"He suspects nothing. Dante is a clever and dangerous man, but he's a predictable child. A fool. Everything will proceed according to plan. In two days the American people will witness the largest massacre ever to occur in their country. At least ten thousand dead. Another thirty thousand injured. The injuries will be particularly severe. The injured will be permanently disfigured."

"Excellent, Zossimov. This will be your most glorious success yet."

"Thank you, sir," Zossimov said with humility in his voice, relieved that his superior could not see the grin on his face. Zossimov had already entered into secret negotiations with his superior's boss. When this project was completed, Zossimov would be promoted into the position of the man he was now talking to. His superior would then be transferred to an unpleasant post somewhere out of sight. Zossimov didn't care where. "Your opinion means so much to me, sir," he said.

"Thank you, Zossimov. You have always been my most successful agent. My favorite. But this time you have achieved a true place for yourself."

Yes, Zossimov thought. *Your* place.

"Good hunting, Zossimov," his superior said. *"Do svidania."*

"Do svidania," Zossimov replied and hung up. He pushed the phone away and rocked back in his TraveLodge motel chair. In two days it would start. And enough blood would flow to wash him into his own office at 2 Dzerzhinsky Square, KGB headquarters. No longer would he just be one of its 700,000 faceless agents. He would be special.

In two days.

When the dead and disfigured would start to be counted.

9

"Can you think of one reason," the redhead frowned, her Mares Sharpshooter spear gun gripped tightly in both hands, "why we shouldn't shish kebab you right now?"

Bolan edged slightly in front of April, protecting her body with his own while making it look as if he was just shifting nervously. He eyeballed each of them, measuring and sizing them the way an undertaker can glance at a corpse and guess its height and weight.

The skinny blond boy held his spear gun too tightly; his fingers were sweating unnaturally.

The redhead was doing the talking, calmly poised between the two men, her shapely freckled legs apart for balance, her hands steady on the spear gun, her eyes nailed to Bolan's. She looked like she knew how to handle herself. She looked like she had pulled triggers before.

It was the tall wiry black man who truly worried Bolan. Cruel eyes raked over him and April, probing and gouging. Deciding. Though he had not yet said a word, it was clear that he was the boss.

"Answer her!" the blond boy demanded, his

voice cracking with nervous tension. "Answer her!"

"Shut up, Baby John," the redhead said. Then she glanced at the black man. "Detroit?"

Detroit squinted at Bolan. His dark face was branded with a handful of tiny white scars that freckled his forehead like a flock of sea gulls. He wore a blue running suit with orange piping down the arms and legs. The matching jacket was unzipped to his navel. He wore nothing beneath it, and Bolan could see another mass of white scars under the sternum.

"I don't like his looks," Detroit said, pivoting and walking away. "Kill them. Now."

Baby John lifted his Mares Frontiersman spear gun to his shoulder and aimed it at April. The redhead swiveled toward Bolan, leveling the tip of her barbed spear at Mack's chest. Behind them, Detroit walked away between shelves of Voit swim fins and snorkels. His feet, in expensive blue Nike running shoes, screeched on the cement floor with each step.

"Money," Bolan called after him.

Detroit hesitated, turned around. "Say what?"

"Money. That's the one reason not to kill us."

Detroit had slowed to a stop, but he did not walk back.

"Me and my friend here are looking for safe passage to the coast," Bolan said. He had an image in his mind of spears sprouting from his and April's chests.

"That so? Well, I ain't Humphrey Bogart, you ain't Ingrid Bergman and this ain't Casablanca. So far you just blowin' smoke up my ass."

"We got your name from a pal. Byron York."

Detroit snorted contemptuously. "That bastard took up with a bunch of faggots out in some forest somewhere. They're busy snorting talcum powder or some shit. You ain't talked *money* yet, sucker."

"He said you might have some use for a few thousand dollars."

"How few?"

Bolan scratched his chin. "Oh, say five thousand."

"Five thousand dollars don't even make me hard."

"What does ten thousand do for you?"

Detroit absently zipped his jacket open and shut a few times. Finally he turned away, crooking a finger over his head. "Bring 'em."

The redhead motioned the Stony warriors forward with her spear gun.

Bolan guided April ahead of him, wedging his body between her and the deadly spears nudging him in the back.

They were led through the two large storage rooms piled high with additional diving equipment, and up a flight of wobbly stairs to a door. Detroit unlocked the dead bolt and entered. Bolan and April followed with heads bowed.

Inside they looked up to see an expensively

decorated three-bedroom apartment that stretched over the entire length of the storage rooms and the store downstairs. Through the muslin curtains that covered the windows of the living room, Bolan could see the street below from which they had entered Davey Jones's Diving Locker.

"Davey Jones, I presume?" Bolan said to Detroit.

"Take a seat, Jack," Detroit sneered.

Bolan and April flopped down on a sofa.

Detroit leaned his spear gun against the wall. "Search them. One funny move and pop a spear through the smartass's balls."

A thin film of sweat glistened along Baby John's upper lip as he pressed the tip of his spear against Bolan's throat and patted him down with one hand. Bolan remained still, studying the kid's weapon. The Mares pneumatic spear gun was one of the best available, 30 percent more powerful than a three-sling rubber gun, and more accurate. It also had a high-low power adjustment switch. Baby John's was set for high.

"This is all," Baby John said at last, holding up the Beretta 93-R rummaged from April's purse.

Detroit smiled like a shark as he sat in a white wicker chair opposite Bolan and April. "Smart weapon. So let's get down to business."

"How much?" Bolan asked.

"For what, exactly?"

"For safe passage to California. We've got a boat connection to make in San Francisco."

Detroit held up his hands. "You misunder stand us, man. We are political, not profit mak ing."

Bolan glanced around the luxurious apartment, nodding at the expensive Sony TV, Pioneer stereo system, Sony VCR. "I can see you're just plain folks."

Detroit grinned mirthlessly. "Just our way of monitoring the enemy's values. Research, brother. If we were a corporation, this would all be tax deductible. Right, Allison?"

The redhead smiled. "In actual fact we'd make out better if we depreciated the equip- ment annually rather than take a straight deduc- tion."

"She's the financial genius around here," Detroit said. "Don't know what we'd do without her. No, sir." He laughed at some private joke.

"Okay, then," Bolan said. "We're willing to make a sizable 'political contribution' to you. That better?"

"How sizable?"

"Twelve thousand. That's our limit."

"You aren't exactly in a bargaining position, Jack. So don't be telling me nothing about god- damn limits."

"I'm telling you what we can afford. Threaten- ing us won't put more money in our pockets."

Detroit tugged his zipper up and down, pursed his lips. "Where'd you get this money? And how come York put you onto us? You don't look like no radicals.''

"We're not," April said. "We're business-persons."

"Business*persons*," Detroit roared. "She speaks for you, man?" he asked Bolan.

"We're a team. We speak for each other."

April spoke. "Let's cut the bullshit, Mr., uh...." She paused, fishing for a name they might later be able to give Hal.

"Lynch. Detroit Lynch. The lady with the brains and legs is Allison Dubin. The kid with the half-assed beard is Johnny Seville, but we call him Baby John, like in that movie."

"West Side Story," April murmured.

Detroit smiled appreciatively. "Yeah, lady. Right. Not bad. Of course, if we decide not to help you, we'll have to kill you. You dig?"

"We knew that before we came here," April said.

"Then you must be real hard up, 'cause right now I'm voting for the kill. And around here I'm the only one with a vote."

"Before you start counting votes, Lynch, think about the money," Bolan said.

"Hey, man, that's the only thing that's keeping you breathing. So start talking. Details, Jack, details."

Bolan glared at Detroit. Then he shrugged. "Not much to tell. I've been in the Army for thirteen years. Haven't been able to get past master sergeant—bust my butt for the service in

Nam and all I get out of it is a Purple Heart and a hearty 'thanks for nothing.' "

"I was in Nam, too, man," Detroit scowled. "So cut the tears and get to the facts. Money."

"Well, I started selling something that belonged to the Army—"

"What? Guns, supplies, jeeps?"

"Much better," April broke in excitedly. "Computer access."

"Is that right?"

"He worked security detail at the camp," she continued, "and I told him what to look for. My background is in computers. Mike here would steal the access codes with a modem hook-up and we'd sell them to people who wanted to use the computers. Then all they had to do was phone in the access code and they could use it as long as they wanted."

Detroit looked over his shoulder at Allison; the young woman was perched in a matching wicker chair, her long legs hooked over the chair's arm, the black tubular spear gun still aimed at Bolan. "Al, can that be done?"

She nodded. "It's possible. They're smart if they pulled it off. Worth millions over the long run."

"Millions. And you only want to give us twelve lousy grand."

"We didn't make millions," Bolan said. "We got caught after a couple months. A pal tipped me off that they were onto me and I grabbed April and we hit the road. AWOL."

Detroit rubbed his hand over the white flecks on his forehead. "What about York? Why'd he send you to us?"

"Because of me," April said. "Byron and I were engaged when we were in college. I knew he still had some connections and I thought he might help. For old times' sake."

"Tugged on the old heartstrings, eh?" Detroit sniggered. "You bitches are all alike." He looked over his shoulder at Allison again. "Whatchya think, Al? These people kosher?"

Allison shrugged. "Sounds reasonable. We could use the bucks."

"Baby John?"

"Why take a chance? Especially now. We kill them and there's no risk."

Detroit laughed. "He's got a point there, folks. But he don't have much of a head for financial matters. His parents own a dozen clothing stores in New Jersey so he still thinks everybody in the world gets an allowance."

"Lay off, Detroit," Baby John protested.

"He thinks this shop actually makes a profit. Let me tell you, it doesn't make enough to keep us in compressed air. But the place works just fine as a front for our little travel agency. And soon there'll be plenty of bucks around. Until then, we still got bills to pay."

"So we've got twelve thousand we're willing to part with now," insisted Bolan. "We make a phone call and it's wired to you immediately."

Detroit shook his head in anger. "Don't rush

me. I got a lot on my mind besides you. It ain't easy being squad leader to a group of cherry grunts. And now we got this special business tonight."

"What special business?" Baby John asked, licking the sweat from his upper lip.

Detroit laughed, zipped his jacket. "A 'numba ten,' buddy boy. You know what that is, Sergeant Rock?"

Bolan nodded. "The worst situation."

"Bingo. Guess you had some time in Nam after all. Ever fire a P-38 while you were there?"

"Only at dinner time."

Detroit cackled harshly. "Okay, okay. You got me there."

"What are you guys talking about?" Baby John asked.

"Nothing you'd know about, boonierat. A P-38 is a collapsible can opener. Collapsed more than it opened. But I guess our Sergeant Rock wasn't no Shake 'n' Bake wonder. He did his time."

"What's all this got to do with that 'numba ten' jazz?" Allison asked.

"Like the man said, Al, it's not Bo Derek. It's the worst."

"What is?"

Detroit laughed again, scratching his white scars as he did so. "You'll see. Tonight. As soon as Dante calls. He has some information he's checking out for us." He faced Bolan and April. "That's when I'll give you my decision—after I

chat with Dante. By then you'll have seen something that will impress you with what happens if
you screw with the Weather Underground.'' He
grinned at April. ''I sure hope you can stand the
sight of blood, lovely lady.'' Then he threw back
his head and laughed obscenely till he shook.

10

The crazies began arriving a couple of hours later.

First came a couple of kids from out of state who were attending Williamsport's Lycoming College. They wore LaCoste shirts and Chaps jeans and carried a bag of groceries each.

With a wink Detroit explained to April loud enough so the boy and girl could hear him, "Part of their admission fee for tonight's entertainment. A couple of virgin honkies who think being radical means wearing their thirty dollar shirts not tucked in."

The college kids set their bags down. The boy started tucking his shirt in.

"Fuck you, Detroit," the girl said, tossing an apple to him.

"You have, Belinda," he said, catching the apple in one hand. He spoke to April again. "Of the two, she's got the bigger balls."

The boy flushed crimson, hefted both bags of groceries and shuffled into the kitchen.

Belinda was a little plump, her blond hair in serious need of washing. A tiny constellation of four gold star earrings lined her left earlobe. The right ear was left bare. "Who're they?" she asked, looking at April and Bolan, her mouth full of apple.

"Customers," Detroit said. "Maybe."

Belinda shrugged and began rummaging through the extensive record collection.

April and Bolan stayed seated on the couch. They had been allowed to get food from the refrigerator and go to the bathroom, but there was always someone right next to them with a weapon.

The spear guns were stacked in a corner next to the TV, replaced by more efficient guns. The redheaded Allison was wielding a Wilkinson Arms Linda—a semiautomatic pistol with an Aimpoint Mark III electronic sight. Loaded with PMC 9mm Luger hardball ammo and fixed with the Aimpoint, even a rank beginner could score an 80-percent hit range.

Baby John toted a Hi-Standard Sentinal Mark IV with a nickel finish, which he pointed at April and Bolan at every opportunity. The sweat on his upper lip had become a permanent fixture despite constant wiping with his sleeve.

Only Detroit Lynch did not have a gun. Instead he wore a belt loaded with five different throwing knives of various sizes. The pockmarked walls of the apartment were a testament to his practice and ability. Particularly a framed reproduction of a portrait of a man in a business suit. The face had been shredded beyond recognition from knives sticking into it. Detroit mentioned that it was a portrait of a former president, though he no longer remembered which one. Now as Detroit paced anxiously about the apartment, he tapped a throwing knife rapidly against his open palm.

"He looks nervous," April whispered to Bolan.

"Yeah. He's waiting for the call from Dante."

"What's that all about, Mack?"

Bolan shrugged. "I don't know. But I don't think it has to do with us. He didn't have a chance to call Dante before he met us."

"It sounded dangerous. Threatening."

"He's getting ready to use those damn toadstickers of his."

A flat blade windmilled between Bolan's and April's faces, thudding into the wall behind them. Paint flecks and plaster snowed like dandruff onto the sofa.

"Quit whispering!" Detroit hollered, veins bulging on his neck, his hand plucking another knife from its sheath.

All sounds in the apartment were hushed.

Bolan twisted the knife out of the wall, hefted it in his palm. "Nice weight," he said. As fast as a striking cobra, he flicked it back toward Detroit. The blade cleared the radical's head by a good four inches before biting into the steer skull in the Georgia O'Keefe poster behind him.

Detroit spun, looked at the knife still quivering slightly, laughed loudly. "Yes, sir, Sergeant Rock. I'm almost gonna be sorry if I vote against you. Almost." He turned away and went into the kitchen for a drink.

Belinda found a Fleetwood Mac record and

flopped it on the stereo. The noise helped cover Bolan and April's conversation.

"You took a bit of a chance there," April said, her hand pushing back her hair, her face anxious, frowning, despite her light tone of voice.

"Not really. Chances are they intend to kill us anyway."

"Mack, is that supposed to make me feel better?"

"We have to wait until we get a line on Dante before we act. Probably right after the phone call. Just hold on tight until then. Can you make it?"

She nodded forcefully. Gratefully.

As each minute ticked by, Detroit began pacing more insistently, glancing at his watch, tugging at his jacket zipper, tapping his knife, scratching his scars. He guzzled two Budweisers, but they did not change his mood.

More people showed up, including a couple of hardcore Weather Underground who had been out delivering weapons. The man wore a torn leather aviator's jacket and packed a Colt .357 in the waist of his beltless cords. The woman was tall and square-shouldered with a chipped front tooth and black hair pulled into a severe pony tail; she waved a Ruger Mark I Bull Barrel .22 around as if it were an extension of her hand. They were in their early thirties.

"You weren't due back for another day," Allison said.

"Yeah. But Dante told us to come over here now, wait for his call."

Bolan watched as Detroit explained the situation to them in the corner of the room, their voices muffled by Belinda's latest selection of Phil Ochs's "Cops of the World." Detroit would occasionally nod toward the prisoners and smile. The newcomers shrugged indifferently as if it hardly mattered whether or not they killed them. Right now they just wanted a beer.

A buzzer sounded, and Baby John was dispatched to admit the latest arrivals through the delivery door downstairs. Minutes later he ushered in two familiar faces.

"Do you know who that is?" April asked.

"Yeah. Dolph Connors, center with the Pittsburgh Steelers."

"Not him. *Her.* That's Carly Carlyle, on one of those soaps."

Bolan grinned at April. "I didn't know you watched."

"I don't and you know it," she snapped. "But her face stares at me from the cover of every tabloid every time I go shopping. What the hell are they doing here?"

"Radical chic. Maybe they feel guilty about all the money they make, so they hang around with radicals. Maybe they think what they do isn't worthwhile. Maybe a lot of things. But there's one thing for sure. They made a mistake coming here tonight."

"Hey, Detroit," Dolph waved happily.

"Shit, man. What happened to you boys last week? Houston handed your asses to you."

Dolph shrugged. "Injuries." Then he went out into the kitchen, yanked open the refrigerator.

"He's a little touchy," Carly explained. "There's been some talk about him not starting this Sunday."

"Tell him not to worry," Detroit laughed. "This Sunday everybody starts."

The soap star sidled up to Detroit, trying to look good to him, managing only cheap. She slipped an arm around his waist. "Who are the stiffs on the sofa?"

Detroit backhanded her in the face.

"Not my face!" she screamed.

Detroit wrapped his long fingers around her throat, tightening his grip as he spoke. "You see these people, Sergeant Rock?" he said to Bolan. "They're what we'd call white trash. Rich kids what need to belong." Blood trickled from the corner of her mouth where he had hit her. Carly Carlyle's face flooded red from his hand around her throat. "Well, ain't you gonna save the bitch?" he said, glancing at Bolan again. "You look like the kind who likes to defend women. Ain't that right, Carly, baby?" He released her throat. She sagged to the floor at his feet, gasping for air. "Well, bitch?"

Carly looked up at Detroit, slowly licked the blood from her mouth and smiled at him. She reached up and kissed his hand. "Just not the face, okay, honey? The makeup people give me hell when I've got a bruise."

Detroit Lynch laughed again and shook his

head at Bolan. "White chicks, man. No wonder you honkies can't get it up."

The jangle of the phone sliced through all conversation.

Detroit moved fast into the kitchen, yelled at everyone there to get out as he snatched up the receiver. From the living room, Bolan could hear only mumbled conversation.

Minutes later Detroit returned, tapping his largest throwing knife in his palm. A cruel smile twisted his lips. "That was Dante," he said unnecessarily. "He's on his way over now."

April shot Bolan a glance.

"He says there's a spy in this place right now." He walked slowly across the room, looking at everyone, his smile frozen, teeth glistening. Finally his gaze rested on Bolan. "Yeah, Dante says one of you mothers is an undercover Fed. Baby John, is your little popgun aimed at our visitors?"

"Yes, Detroit."

"Allison, you got 'em covered real good with that thing?"

"Yes."

He crossed the lush carpet and stood between Allison and Bolan. "Good. We don't want anybody making any sudden moves. Except, of course, me—" And he pivoted around with the heavy metal handle of his throwing knife sizzling the air like a blackjack as it crushed the high chiseled cheekbone of Allison Dubin's face. With his left hand he jerked the Linda from her hand and clubbed her again with the knife handle, this time mashing the back of the hand held up desperately to protect her wounds.

Belinda screamed and Carly whimpered. Everyone else just stared.

Except Allison. She crumbled to the floor, her face swollen with red knots, her hand bleeding and limp.

Detroit stood over her, eyes wide and fierce, chest heaving with excitement. "Now you're gonna find out what we do to cops around here, scum. By the time we're done with you, you ain't gonna be a woman. Hell, you ain't even gonna be human."

11

"Keep the gag real tight!" Detroit yelled at Baby John. "We don't want the bitch screaming and bringing in the whole goddamn neighborhood."

Baby John tugged the dishtowel tighter, jerking Allison's head back sharply as he tied the knot. She was bound to the wicker chair with thick yellow rope from the store downstairs. The left side of her face was puffy around a bony white lump, stretching her skin so taut across her cheek that the freckles disappeared. Her left eye was swollen shut.

"Gonna teach you a little lesson." Detroit laughed. He raised the point of the throwing knife to Allison's face, ran it lightly across her forehead, circled her one good eye.

Belinda and her college friend wore sickly pale expressions as they sat cross-legged in the corner.

The two hardcases that Dante had sent were sitting at the dining-room table sharing a bucket of Kentucky Fried Chicken. They watched Detroit with dead eyes, occasionally licking their fingers and grinning.

Dolph Connors sipped his fifth can of beer. His eyes were slightly blurry, his lips were loose.

Carly, the soap star, squirmed with delighted anticipation. She watched the whole scene like a starving woman devouring a feast.

Bolan and April sat quietly on the sofa. Waiting.

Occasionally they spoke, whispering beneath the noise of the stereo.

"What about Allison?" April said, her head down.

"She's a trained agent. I hope she can hold out until Dante gets here."

"And if she can't?"

Bolan fell silent. There was nothing he could do except mentally construct his death list. But when the time came, first Detroit, then Dante. The more he got to know these people, the longer that hit list would grow.

Detroit leaned down, his face inches from Allison's. He bared his teeth in a repulsive grin. "Well, I guess I know why you were always so prim when I tried to make it with you. I thought you were a dike. Now I find out you're a Fed."

She stared back through her one open eye. Pain clenched her damaged face, but her eye gleamed with defiance. Broken but not bowed; Bolan noted her attitude with admiration.

"Any time now, J.D. Dante will be struttin' through that door, baby. And he ain't gonna treat you nice like me. He can get real *mean*." Detroit ran the tip of his knife along her bare inner thigh to the hem of her shorts. Tiny white scratches etched into her freckled skin. "The thing is, sweets, you're gonna talk sooner or later. The only question is, how much irreparable damage will there be when it's over?" He nodded at Baby John, who quickly removed the dishtowel gag. "Now, it would look good to my boss, ole J.D., if I already had the information before he got here. You dig? So maybe you can tell me how much you passed on to your piggy buddies?"

"I didn't have a chance to report in yet," Allison muttered. "Not since last month."

Detroit shook his head, began tapping the point of his knife on the knob of her broken cheek. She winced from the touch. "That's jive, bitch."

"No, it isn't," she insisted. "We only report in once a month when we're on deep cover. That's standard."

"She's right," Bolan said. "I worked Army intelligence once. That's the way our spy book read. Once a month in deep cover, depending on the length of the operation."

Detroit spun around, spraying saliva as he yelled, "Shut your hole, Jack. I ain't talking to you. You got your own problems to worry about."

"Just being helpful," Bolan smiled.

Detroit turned back to Allison, his fingers walking along her leg, across her thigh, pressing into her crotch. He made a fist and leaned his weight roughly into her.

Her mouth opened with pain, but she wisely made no sound. Sweat beaded along her forehead.

Baby John chewed on his lip as he watched excitedly. Carly urged Detroit on with her eyes. Dolph stared drunkenly. The college kids looked scared. The hardcases argued over an extra-crispy drumstick.

"I want answers!" Detroit screamed into her face, his nose pressed against hers. "What did you report?"

She shook her head.

Then the cutting began.

"A throwing knife ain't very sharp," he said as he moved the blade. "But it's got a decent point. It'll do."

And he began gouging furrows of skin from her face. First a strip from her good cheek. Blood welled from the two-inch wound, dripping down her chin onto her T-shirt. Then he dragged it cross her busted cheek and she swooned. More blood splashed down her face.

Bolan felt April's fingers flexing around his arm. He glanced at his watch. There was no telling where Dante had phoned from, how long it would take him to arrive. If Dante was in another town it could take an hour through the winding Pennsylvania roads. But by then, if Allison was still alive, she'd wish she wasn't.

Bolan assessed the tactical situation.

The college kids were unarmed and were in too much shock to do anything anyway. The celebrities were just as useless. Baby John had his Sentinal, but Detroit and Allison were in the line of fire to Bolan. The hardcases at the dining-room table had their guns tucked in their waist-bands, but they were bellied-up to the table, their fingers greasy with chicken. They'd have to push themselves back to get at the guns, and that would take precious seconds. Life and death seconds.

Detroit had his throwing knives and he knew how to use them. And lying on the wicker coffee table less than five feet in front of him was Allison's Wilkenson Arms Linda with the Aim-point.

Bolan nudged April. He pointed surreptitious-ly with his chin at the Linda laying on the wicker table. He raised his eyebrows to ask if she could handle the weapon. She studied it a mo-ment, barely nodded. Then he nodded slightly, too.

Detroit dug his knife into Allison's skin again and Bolan and April bolted off the sofa in different directions. While April lunged across the living room for the semiauto-matic pistol, Bolan dived over the side of the couch into the corner where the spear guns were leaning.

He was raising the Sharpshooter at the same time Baby John was aiming his Sentinel at April's back.

Bolan squeezed the trigger and the spear leaped from the gun, zipped across the room and punched through Baby John's skinny neck. The guy's eyes bulged as his hands flew to the shaft, trying to tug it out.

But the hinged barbs had flattened against the back of his neck, anchoring the spear permanently in place.

He spiraled to the ground, his hands still wrapped uselessly around the shaft. He was dead.

The hardcases at the dining-room table pushed themselves backward, grabbing at their guns. But April had snatched up the Linda and was slinging a dozen rounds of 9mm hardballs at them.

Brass casings piled up around her feet as the bullets gnarled the table, two chairs, and the thigh, hip and ribs of the guy at the table.

The woman somersaulted back into the kitchen and closed the door. April tossed another half-dozen rounds through it to keep the woman out of the way.

The college kids were huddled against each other, flat against the floor, their faces buried in thick shag carpeting. Belinda was screaming. Dolph sat uncomprehending, his mouth hanging open stupidly. Carly's eyes sparkled with frenzy.

But it was Detroit who had Bolan worried. As soon as Baby John dropped, the crazed fanatic spun and snapped his throwing knife at the black-suited nightfighter. The blade sliced air with a high-pitched whistle, missing Bolan's head by a hair.

Bolan tossed aside the spent Sharpshooter and hooked the Frontiersman, aiming and firing in less than two seconds.

It was enough time for Detroit to yank Carly in front of him. Enough time for the rocketing spear to drill through the actress's abdomen, soaking her expensive Ralph Lauren sweater with her blood.

She pitched forward, slammed facedown on the floor. The shaft was driven all the way through her body.

Detroit scrambled toward the dining-room table for the dead man's gun. April stitched the last row of 9mm peepholes into the kitchen door, then in one movement swung the Linda around at Detroit as Bolan hefted the last spear gun. They both fired simultaneously.

The spear caught Detroit square in the chest, just above where his jacket zipper stopped and bare skin began. April was less generous. She started low and fired a burst from crotch to neck and back down again. Detroit's pulpy body flew up against the wall, splotched the paint with flecks of bloody flesh and cloth, then flopped onto the carpet. It twitched in death.

April had already untied Allison and was helping her to her feet.

"You should have waited for Dante," she gasped with agony. "Gotten them all."

"We didn't have your guts," Bolan said. "Let's get out of here before the cops come."

They started toward the door, stepping over corpses, wading through pools of guts and blood. Each had an arm around Allison as they half-dragged her with them. On the way, Bolan dug his

Beretta 93-R out of the credenza drawer where Detroit had tossed it, then trained it on the kitchen door. "If you know what's smart," he called through the door, "you'll stay put and live."

April fumbled with the front door, opened it, began edging Allison through.

Dolph Connors stood up, staggered forward a couple steps. "Hey, man," he demanded belligerently. "What about me?"

Bolan lifted the Beretta slightly and squeezed off a round into the floor between Dolph's legs. The impact raised dust and a couple of tiny splinters. The shocked football player imagined he had sustained some sort of wound to his precious legs, whose knees had already seen so much surgery. He sank moaning to the floor.

"You ought to be selling used cars," Bolan muttered. It appalled him that reckless idiots strayed into his appointed path and bared themselves up as victims to him. No man was more truly merciful than a soldier like Mack Bolan who had lived on the edge of creation and brought back gifts of compassion for mankind and the gift of mercy for each individual. Victims who put themselves wilfully into the cross fire, begging for a lesson they'd not forget, only distracted a soldier from his path, although the lesson must always be taught in full.

Belinda was screaming. The college boy pressed his hand against her mouth to silence her.

Bolan thought about saying something to them, some piece of counsel for their lives. But he shrugged instead and ushered Allison and April down the stairs. They were old enough to learn for themselves. If, after everything they had seen tonight, they still had a taste for the radical life, then so be it. He would see them again someday, probably through the sights of his Beretta.

They were halfway down the stairs when they heard a car pull up outside the rear of the building. Three car doors slammed. The buzzer sounded upstairs in the apartment.

"Front door," Bolan whispered. "Through the store."

Allison was running under her own strength now, keeping up with April, holding a rag carefully against her bleeding face. Bolan backed out after them, his Beretta covering their escape.

"Keep going," he told them. "I'll catch up later."

April's expression was concerned, but she nodded reluctantly. She and Allison ducked through the fishing net and out of sight. They would be out the front door and safe within minutes.

But Bolan still had business here. Maybe he had screwed up the mission in order to save Allison, but it had been necessary. "For what is a man profited, if he shall gain the whole world, and lose his own soul?"

Mack Bolan knew that Allison's life was not his to sacrifice. Saving her was what he was all about. Saving her and every good soul like her.

He edged around one of the metal shelves

stacked with low-pressure compressors. He hunched down in the dark room and waited.

The buzzer sounded a couple more times, an impatient finger jabbing it outside. Then heavy footsteps thundered down the wooden stairs. Bolan peered around the shelf.

It was the woman who had hid in the kitchen. She quickly unlocked the back door and began frantically explaining as the three men entered.

Bolan recognized the pale angry face of J.D. Dante.

"Slow down, dammit!" he snapped, shaking her shoulders. "What's going on here? Where's Detroit?"

"Dead," she panted, barely able to catch her breath. "So's Baby John and that soap bitch. And Billy. They killed them all."

"Who, the Fed?"

She nodded. "She and the couple Byron York sent."

"I *told* Detroit to keep an eye on them! Where are they now?" Dante boomed.

She pointed out the front door.

Dante spun around and shoved his two soldiers in that direction. "Go after them! Kill them!"

The two men tugged their Colt MK V Troopers out of concealed holsters. They ran through the dark storage room and out the front door.

Dante raked his thick hair with his fingers. "Any of them know anything?"

"I don't know how they would," the woman

said. "None of us knew anything to spill except that it's going down Sunday."

"Good. That's all you need to know. Zossimov has everything set up, regardless of the shit that's going down here. If the weather holds and the smog's not too bad, we'll have half a million people on target."

"Jesus," she whispered.

"And that's just the beginning," he bragged, as if to talk himself out of bad news. "That little caper will set off a chain reaction of bombings and attacks that'll make the Weather Underground more talked about than *E.T.*"

The woman looked around. "Where's Bleeder?"

"C'mon, you don't think I'd actually bring that asshole here, do you? He's good for money, some laughs, a safehouse, that's all." He pointed up. "Anybody else upstairs?"

"A couple of college kids, the football player."

"They alive?"

"The kids are okay. But the big man who busted Allison out of here, he scared Dolph all to hell, told him to start selling used cars."

Dante laughed arrogantly, rocking slightly. "Hell, I'd like to meet this guy."

The woman sighed. "I don't think so, J.D. Something about him.... You had to see him move. The bastard speared Baby John and Detroit. Carly got in the way and he speared her, too. The chick snatched up that Linda and split Billy and Detroit open like eggs."

"Then get upstairs and finish off the others. We don't want any witnesses talking."

She started up the stairs, her Ruger clutched in her right hand.

A siren wailed nearby.

Dante spat in disgust. "I'll get the car started." He turned and moved out the back door.

The woman scampered up the last few stairs as Bolan sprang out from behind the shelf and chugged several 9mm parabellums into her side. The impact whirled her around, yanked her off the stairs and through the wooden railing.

Her body belly-flopped into a metal shelf half-filled with boxes of fins and wet suits. She knocked the shelf over as she fell face first against the cement floor. Blood puddled around her crushed face.

The car outside roared loudly as tires screamed across pavement. Dante was getting the hell out.

Bolan had no more intention of getting picked up by the police than Dante did, so he dashed through the room and out the front door, tracing the path he suspected April and Allison had taken.

The dark streets were deserted. There were no residential homes, only small businesses, offices and a bank. That was why it had taken so long for someone to call the police.

Bolan ran silently, his footsteps no more than a sigh as he paced through the alleys looking for April and Allison. And for the two gunmen following them.

Ahead of him, a distant burst of gunfire, a

couple of single shots, another burst.... Then silence.

He ducked between the post office and a drug store, following the sound. Behind him he heard several sirens wailing as patrol cars screeched up to the diving store.

Bolan ran across Third Street. He made no effort to hide his weapon in the deserted street. Bolan had seen plenty of towns like Williamsport before. The sidewalks rolled up after five o'clock and no one was seen again until seven o'clock the next morning.

As he hit the curb on the other side of the street, he knew he was on the right track. Propped up against the wall of a Thrifty Loan office door was a man, his head hanging down, his legs sprawled out like a drunk's. Enough to fool most people. Except Bolan had seen him with Dante a few minutes earlier. The man was dead.

Carefully Bolan edged around the corner of the building into a dark alley. It was like a tunnel. He took two steps before his foot nudged another body. He flipped the corpse over, grimly acknowledged the features. Dante's other gunman. Bullet holes had chewed a hunk of flesh from his chest.

Bolan trotted down the alley. "April?"

A gray figure peeled away from the shadows, stepped into a spear of light from a street lamp. April. He had not known how truly anxious he was about her until that second.

She held him, then they turned to gently lift Allison to her feet.

"The target?" Allison gasped, her teeth clenched in pain.

"They didn't identify it."

April cursed.

"But I think I know what it is," Bolan said. "If I'm right, we have to move fast. Or God help a whole mass of innocent victims."

12

"You sure about the location?" The Fed chewed his soggy cigar and sighed. "Scratch that question."

"Fair question, Hal," Bolan said on the phone. "But I gave you the facts just as I got them. Dante hoped the good weather would hold. It's been raining in northern California for the past week. That combined with his comment about smog suggests Southern California. And they specified Sunday. What's going down on Sunday that involves half a million people?"

"The OPON Festival," Brognola replied. "One People One Nation. A twenty-million-dollar country-and-western festival in Riverdale. The TV news has been showing the crowds that have been gathering there since Wednesday. And the gates didn't even open until this morning. Make that yesterday morning. It's twelve minutes into Saturday already."

Bolan peered through the glass phone booth at April. She sat in the front seat of the car, her head leaning against the headrest, her eyes closed.

"I'll say one thing for Dante and Zossimov," continued Brognola, speaking from Stony Man

Farm. "They picked the best day for it. By the end of Friday there were about two hundred forty thousand people attending. By Sunday, they expect half a million. That's when the really big names appear. Willie Nelson, Waylon Jennings, the Oak Ridge Boys, Alabama, Fleetwood Mac and Linda Ronstadt."

"Which means the stars will be targets as well as the audience."

"Have to be. There's no way to be selective with that size of a crowd." Brognola paused. "How's Sally Benson doing?"

"A.k.a. Allison Dubin? She's fine. We put her in Divine Providence Hospital and they've patched her up. There'll be some nasty scars on her face, but the doctor said plastic surgery can take care of that. With luck."

"Seems that around the time she was being admitted," continued Hal, "a certain football player was being checked into the Williamsport Hospital with some sort of nervous condition. Doesn't look like he'll be playing pro ball very well for a while."

Bolan shrugged. "It's a tough game," he responded.

"That's what I said."

"You come up with anything on Bleeder?"

"Not yet. I've run the name through the computer. Spelled it several different ways. I'm still waiting for the results." A deep puff on the cigar. "One question, Mack."

"Sure."

"Why didn't you kill Dante when you had the chance?"

Bolan peered through the glass again, watched April wriggle in her seat. Then she opened her eyes, glanced around for him, waved to him through the windshield. He waved back. "Believe me, Hal, there's nothing I wanted to do more than nail that bastard's flesh to the wall. But when I heard him say that Zossimov had everything set up already, I knew I had to wait. If I'd blown Dante away, chances are good that Zossimov would have continued the operation without Dante. At least with him alive, we have a chance of picking up his trail and tracing him to Zossimov. We have to find out how they intend to attack that many people."

"The whole thing's crazy, Mack. The place will be crawling with security guards, not to mention the audience itself. The place is swept twice a day for bombs. They even have air surveillance. How are they going to do it?"

"Beats me. All I know is that I'm not going to let it happen."

Brognola sighed wearily. "Hang by that phone a few more minutes. I'll call back as soon as the computer's regurgitated its dinner."

Bolan hung up.

April opened the car door. She climbed out and stretched. "What's the word from Hal?"

"He thinks they're going to strike a music festival, a big one, at Riverdale, near L.A."

She walked over to Bolan, slid her arm around his waist. He rested his hand on her shoulder, then hugged her close against him. They leaned up against the fender of the car and watched the vehicles shooting by on Route 15 like flaming meteors. Next to them was a 24-hour doughnut shop with one customer, a Valley Farms dairy truck driver. The waitress was leaning over the counter reading the newspaper.

April spoke at last. "People listening to music, enjoying each other. And those animals are going to use that opportunity to kill people. Just to make some obscure political point."

The phone in the glass booth rang.

Bolan started for it. If Hal had the information they needed, there would still be a chance to stop the slaughter. If not. . . .

13

Larry "The Bleeder" Strohman was running scared. As he bounced through the house with his nylon Sports Sac traveling bag slung over his shoulder, he grabbed any object he passed and threw it in. Some clothes, a couple of paperback mysteries, sunglasses, broken pen. He just couldn't think very straight.

Dante was supposed to have been back two hours ago. He had taken Bleeder's car and rounded up two other toughs and sped off for Williamsport, laughing about what he would do to that undercover Fed. But there was still no sight of him, not even a phone call. What if something had gone wrong? The cops might be on their way here right now!

He had to get out. Hide. His sister would let him stay in her mountain cabin, as long as her husband Tom didn't know. Tom did not like Bleeder. But then neither did Bleeder's sister.

He jogged into his study on unsteady legs and began rifling through the rolltop desk. He stuffed his wallet into his pocket and clamped his address book between his teeth while he crammed a checkbook into the bulging bag.

That's when he heard the explosion.

At least it sounded like an explosion. The loud disintegration of wood was shattering to him. He stood, frozen in motion, teeth chomping into the soft leather address book. Bile rose in his throat.

Bolan plunged through the doorway. Garbed in blacksuit, the Beretta 93-R held at arm's length in double fists, his presence was undeniable. The dark hole of the barrel stared hungrily at Bleeder's forehead.

Bleeder's mouth dropped open, the address book tumbled to the floor. It was a judgment from heaven and a punishment from hell all staring at him from those icy eyes.

"In here, April," Bolan called out. April appeared seconds later after checking the other rooms. The Linda semiautomatic pistol was gripped in both hands like a submachine gun.

"Doesn't seem to be anyone else here," she said.

"Just us chickens," Bolan said to Bleeder.

Bleeder dropped his bag. Something inside shattered. "How'd you get in here?" he croaked.

"We busted your door down, that's how."

"What do you want?"

"Dante!"

Bleeder recoiled from Bolan's shout, stumbling backward a couple of steps into the desk. "Who are you? Cops?"

"We're the ones with the questions. And the guns."

"Where's your warrant?"

"I'm about to perforate your lungs with it."

Bleeder shook so much he groped behind him for the desk chair. He swiveled it around and collapsed in it. He crossed his legs in an effort to hide his wet pant leg.

Bolan walked over to him and pressed the cold muzzle against Bleeder's forehead. "Last time, pal. Where's Dante? The operation at Davey Jones's is busted. Where would he go next? How would he get out to California?"

Bleeder gaped at Bolan, shocked by how much the stranger knew. A trickle of blood bubbled from one nostril. He sniffed it back in. "I don't know anything," he whined, his voice pinched with fear. "Go ahead and shoot. Kill me. Go ahead."

Bolan swore to himself. From what little Hal Brognola had been able to tell him about this creep, he had always been self-destructive, a wimp, bullied by everyone in his life, especially the Weather Underground. Just their luck that for once in his life the punk decides to become a political hero, preferring to take a bullet than talk.

Damn, they didn't have the time for this. Eventually Bleeder would talk, given the right combination of pain. But Bolan did not have that much time.

"Listen to me, Strohman," Bolan threatened.

"Sir," April interrupted. "May I see you a moment?"

Bolan nodded grudgingly, backed up until he stood next to her.

"You agree that fear is more effective than the pain?" she whispered.

"Sometimes."

She smiled at him and handed him her gun. "I'll be right back. Need something from my purse." She dashed out the door. Bolan glared icily at Bleeder, both barrels hovering at the guy's heart. April returned in less than a minute. Her right hand was balled into a fist as she walked toward Bleeder. When she stood in front of him, she thrust out her hand and opened it. Bleeder flinched at the movement.

Sitting on her palm was a white oblong pill.

"Swallow this," she ordered harshly.

"Wh-what is it?"

"Never mind. Just do it. Unless you'd prefer my friend to start using his knife on your privates."

Bleeder shivered. Reluctantly he picked up the pill and turned it in his hand like a strange jewel. Finally he squared his shoulders and popped the pill into his mouth and swallowed it.

April glanced at her watch. "You have five minutes. It'll seem much longer because of the nature of the chemicals."

"Chemicals?"

"Same basic ingredients your Soviet buddies use in Yellow Rain. It makes your blood vessels burst. Soon you'll feel a hot rush on your skin, which happens right before the blood starts to seep through your pores. It means your internal organs are dissolving."

Sweat beads bloomed across Bleeder's face.

"Now, where's Dante?"

"Why should I tell you anything?" he groaned. "I'm dying anyway."

"Because of this." She pulled an orange oblong pill from her pocket. "The antidote. It completely reverses the process."

"I—I can feel my skin tingling already," he gasped. "Feels hot and burning."

"A little ahead of schedule," she shrugged, bouncing the orange pill in her palm. "It's just a matter of minutes now."

Blood oozed from his nostril. He swiped at it with his hand, stared at the smear. "It's worse than usual," he said hysterically. "Thicker."

Bolan looked at his watch. He nodded at April. "Let's go. He's not going to talk."

"Guess you're right," she said as she pocketed the orange pill.

"Royce Banjo!" Bleeder blurted out.

April spun back to face him. "What about him? He's a country singer."

"That's where Dante would have gone next. At least, that was his plan." Bleeder wiped frantically at his nose, sobs racking his skinny frame. "Royce is sympathetic to our cause and agreed to give J.D. cover as a roadie with his band. He's giving J.D. a lift on his chartered jet. They're probably on their way to Los Angeles by now. Royce is supposed to play at that phony Woodstock, the OPON Festival."

"What do you know about OPON?" Bolan asked.

"Nothin'."

Bolan stared at him a moment, watching the fear shake his body. Bolan decided the punk meant it. "Okay," he said to April.

April tossed Bleeder the orange pill, which he caught with both hands and quickly swallowed. His throat was so dry it took several gulps to get it down.

Then Bolan lashed Bleeder to a water pipe that ran down the wall of the room. A call to Brognola would ensure that someone would be by to pick him up and keep him out of circulation for a while.

"Just what was it you gave him back there?" Bolan asked April. They were speeding toward a military airbase. Hal had arranged for them to hitchhike a jet ride to California. "Whatever it was, it sure did the trick."

"Niacin," she smiled. "Available from the drug store. I take it sometimes with my vitamins. High-potency Niacin opens your pores, gives you a flushed feeling. Perfectly harmless, but it can be scary if you've never taken it before."

"Then what was the 'antidote'?"

"Vitamin C. Want one? Tasty."

Bolan laughed as he wheeled the car through the sparse early-morning traffic.

14

"How do I look?" she teased, striking a model's pose that showed her full curves to their best advantage, her warm smile bright with intelligence.

Bolan pointed through the windshield at the guests streaming into the large house. "Better than anybody here."

"Considering the cost of some of those outfits, I'll take that as a compliment. You know, this is the first party you've ever taken me to."

"Oh, yeah, how about Hal's birthday party a couple of months ago?"

"I mean outside of Stony Man Farm. Besides, I arranged that whole party, you didn't take me."

"Close enough."

"Boy, do you have a lot to learn about women."

"How much?"

She smiled at him. "Not much."

His eyes remained fixed straight ahead, studying the guests as they parked their cars and ran laughing into the large Spanish-style house in the Brentwood Hills. The sound of a live band rippled through the night.

Bolan and April Rose had taken advantage of

down time on the jet flight to catch some sleep, though neither felt really refreshed at the moment. It was 9:21 P.M. on the Saturday night before the massacre planned for Sunday.

Bolan knew no details yet, but he knew it would be a massacre. That was Zossimov's specialty, his gospel. And in Dante, Zossimov must have found the perfect disciple in death.

Royce Banjo's fame as an "outlaw" country singer made it easy to track him down. Brognola had ordered surveillance of Banjo's chartered jet when it landed. But if there was one thing celebrities were good at, it was losing whoever was following them. Most had specially trained bodyguard-drivers able to shake them free from adoring fans or potential kidnappers. It was the only way most could get any privacy. Royce Banjo was no exception. His limo, containing himself and Dante, had left the two FBI agents scratching their heads somewhere on Pico Boulevard.

It had taken some legwork, but the party tonight was not much of a secret. The house was rented for Royce Banjo by his record label. The caterers had arrived several hours ago, followed by the band and finally the guests. But still no sign of Banjo. Or Dante.

"Do you think he'd throw a party and not come to it?" April drummed her fingernails on the dashboard.

"That's what being an 'outlaw' means. Breaking rules."

"Maybe there's some other way in."

"There is," Bolan pointed. "He'd have to climb down the hill there through that patch of woods. Not likely."

"Sometimes these parties go on all night, even a couple of days."

"Yeah, we had a couple parties like that in Saigon."

"I mean he might not show up for hours, if at all."

Bolan nodded. "I know." He looked at his watch. "And we can't keep waiting here. Let's go."

"What?"

"Let's go in and ask some questions."

April watched him get out of the car and shrug into a corduroy sports jacket from the trunk. He fastened the middle button, partially concealing his blacksuit.

"You look like a record producer," she said. "It's the suede patches on the elbows, I think."

Bolan jammed the Beretta in his waistband at the hollow of his back and motioned to April. "Come on, you party animal. Let's boogie."

There was no one at the door to question them; it wasn't that kind of party. In fact, the front door was wide open, allowing people to flow freely. The crush of bodies generated waves of thick heat. That and the heavy cloying scent of marijuana made the rooms seem even smaller.

The band was playing "Take This Job and Shove It" in the next room; the vibrations from the amplifiers rattled the framed movie posters on the walls. The steady din of several hundred people talking, laughing and singing at once made normal conversation impossible.

Bolan cupped his hands around his mouth and pressed them close to April's ear. "Ask around for one of Royce's band."

She nodded, made an okay sign with thumb and finger, and started tapping men on the shoulders. It took a few times and a lot of propositions before she finally found someone who pointed out Royce's bass-guitar player.

"Over there!" she shouted into Bolan's ear. "The big one in the Lakers jacket and cowboy hat."

Bolan held April's hand and moved through the tight crowd. Drugs were being openly exchanged, including small vials of cocaine. Wearing only black bikini panties and a bow tie, a pretty young woman was dancing in the middle of a circle. A man in a rhinestone tuxedo was vomiting in the pot of a six-foot-tall rubber tree in the hallway.

Moving through the crowd was like being swallowed by a python, Bolan thought. The throng swelled and constricted like the throat muscles of the snake, urging the doomed animal deeper into the stomach. At one point the crowd slammed shut between Bolan and April and he had to yank her roughly through.

At last they stood before the bass player, Tim Manton, as Bolan recalled from Hal's briefing. Manton was a few inches shorter than Bolan, but fifty pounds heavier, most of it settled around his gut. A thick leather belt girdled his stomach, fastened by a huge silver buckle that said, "Rock 'n' Roll Must Die!"

He had a can of Coors in one beefy hand, the other was wrapped around the shoulder of a skinny girl about sixteen years old. Her lipstick was smeared onto her chin and she giggled constantly.

"Tim Manton?" Bolan asked.

"Yup." Manton adjusted his towering cowboy hat, battered and stained with sweat. He guzzled the rest of his Coors and handed the can to the young girl. "Get me another, babe."

"Sure, Tim." She giggled and ran off.

"What can I do you for, partner?"

Bolan smiled, looked cautiously around before offering his hand. "Jim Melville, RCA."

Danton's eyes lit up. "Nice to meet you, Jim."

"This probably isn't the right time, but, hell, my little darlin' here thinks you're terrific."

"Just love you," April added shyly.

"Thanks, ma'am. We got the best band in C&W, I think."

"Oh, yes, the band's great. But we're talking about you specifically."

Manton beamed. "Me?"

The little sixteen-year-old trotted up like a colt, another can of Coors held out for him. "Here you go, Tim."

Manton snatched it from her. "Get lost, babe. I'll see you later. The grown-ups are talkin' business here."

She winced from his harshness, faded back into the crowd without a word.

"We are talkin' business, ain't we?" Manton asked Bolan.

Bolan smiled. "Well, I don't want to be accused of raiding any label's artists. That's unethical."

"Yeah, sure. But hypothetically, what's the deal?"

Bolan looked around again. "Is there somewhere a little more private?"

"Can't get much more privacy than the middle of this crowd," Manton bellowed, his stomach shaking with laughter.

"I don't like talking six-figure amounts in the middle of a crowd."

Manton's eyes widened. He licked his thick blubbery lips. "Right this way, Mr. RCA."

He guided them through the crowd, bulling his way to the stairs. Bolan and April followed him up the elaborate winding staircase to the second floor.

"This is Royce's bedroom," Manton said, opening the door.

Inside, a naked couple bounced on the bed. The man had gray wavy hair and a guitar tattooed on his right shoulder. The girl was the one who had been dancing topless downstairs. She still wore her bow tie around her neck.

Manton dug his foot under the pile of clothes next to the bed and kicked them into the air. They fluttered onto the startled couple. "Get the hell outta here, Gordy. Take the baggage with you."

"Sorry, Tim," Gordy said sheepishly, grabbing most of the clothes with one hand and the girl with the other.

Manton booted the door closed behind them and grinned slyly at Bolan. "Just blowin' off steam before we play at that OPON Festival tomorrow."

"I'm looking forward to catching your act there. By the way, where's Royce tonight?"

Manton shrugged massive shoulders. "Who knows? He's got his own friends. Now just what exactly is that six-figure amount you mentioned downstairs."

"Four hundred thousand. Maybe five hundred thousand."

Manton stared numbly. "Dollars?"

"No," Bolan said. "People."

"What? I don't get you."

Bolan's voice went harder. "Where's Royce?"

Manton stared at Bolan, saw April backing up to cover the door. "What's goin' on here?"

"An exchange. Your life for Royce's whereabouts."

"Fuck you, amigo." Manton started to brush past Bolan.

Bolan's movements were so fluid, yet so powerful, it was like being hit by a tidal wave. Balance, speed and power united in a molten movement that slammed into Manton at a place—and a time, timing is everything—that ensured the slob would topple. When it was over, Manton was on the floor on his back, Bolan was straddling his chest.

Manton's left hand was being bent at a painful angle by the Executioner.

"Where's Royce?"

"He didn't tell me. We got in at the airport and he took off with that asshole he hired at the last minute. I told him we didn't need another roadie, but he's the goddamn boss."

"Last time, fatty. Where?"

"I don't know. Honest to God, man."

Bolan grabbed Manton's fat pinky finger and snapped it back. Manton's howl failed to cover the cracking noise.

"You broke it! Jesus, man, I can't play the guitar like this. Jesus."

"You've got four more fingers on this hand, then I start on the next. That means I ask nine more times. After the tenth time, well, you'd rather not know."

Tears of pain spilled from Manton's eyes. "Okay, okay. He'll fire me if he finds out I told you, man."

"Where?" Bolan asked again, calmly.

"I've got a phone number, that's all. He left it in case his agent calls. He's got some goddamn movie deal in the works, one that doesn't include the rest of us and—"

"What's the number?"

Manton recited it. "I don't know where he is, though," he added bitterly, grimacing in pain. "He's been hangin' out with his politico buddies lately. All the guys have bad breath and the chicks have mustaches. You know the type. . . ."

Bolan climbed off Manton's chest, whipped out his Beretta and poked it into Manton's stomach. "You don't look too well, Tim. I think the stress of show business is getting to you. If I were you, I'd go have that finger taken care of. Then I'd rent a nice quiet motel room and stay there for twenty-four hours. I wouldn't make any phone calls. That would cause stress. And stress kills. I promise you. Understand?"

"Yes, sir," Manton said, not moving.

ONE PHONE CALL and forty minutes later April and Mack were parked off a dirt road in Laurel Canyon, staring up a slight hill to the single house nestled in the trees at the top. Lights flickered in all the windows, but the only sound was the breeze filtering through the trees.

Bolan flipped open the trunk of their rented Trans Am, reached into the yawning darkness and plucked out the Linda with the Aimpoint. He handed it to April. "Help yourself to the extra clips," he said, nodding at the trunk. "Courtesy of the United States Air Force."

"Nice bunch," April commented as she stuffed the military webbing with clips. "First they fly us out here, then they supply us with ammo, grenades, the works. I wonder how many arms Hal had to twist."

Bolan did not answer. The weapons came as they may. He snapped the folding stock onto the butt of the Beretta and strapped the military webbing that dangled with grenades.

April smeared greasy camouflage cosmetics on her face, then checked over her weapon. "Do you think Dante's up there too?"

"I don't know. I hope so. But even if he isn't, Royce Banjo is. And he'll talk."

She took a deep breath, clutched her gun. "We're getting real good at crashing parties."

Bolan nodded as he smeared some coloring on a spot she missed behind her ear. "Only this time it's going to be party *crushing*."

They crouched low and started up the hill.

15

The first guard hunkered in the tall thistle weeds less than fifteen yards away, trying to light the tiny stub of a once-impressive marijuana joint. His rifle, a Charter Arms Ar-7 Explorer .22, lay in the wet grass beside him. He held the joint carefully between thumb and forefinger, sensitive to the danger of lighting such a short butt.

"C'mon, baby," he muttered under his breath as he struck the wooden match against a protruding rock. His match flared briefly, and with practiced movements he touched the tip of the joint to the flame and sucked in a lungful of bittersweet smoke.

The smoke was still swirling around his lungs when Bolan's wire garrote bit into his throat, cutting off the passageway. The marijuana smoke burned inside the guard's chest, making him more desperate to exhale than to inhale. The guy clawed at the wire, raking off strips of his own skin with his fingernails, but it had already sunk too deep into his flesh. His fingers couldn't dig under it. Then he saw his own blood as it squirted from the razor-thin wound circling his neck. By the time the wire severed his carotid artery, he was dead.

Bolan unwound the garrote and let the body slump silently forward. Even in the dim moonlight he could see the marijuana smoke seeping like steam from the gaping slash in the throat.

Bolan waved and April scurried through the weeds to his side. "One down," Bolan said.

She glanced at the dead man, gritted her teeth. "Let's do it."

The house was another fifty feet up the hill. The only cover for Bolan and April was the field of knee-high thistle weeds, but the house itself was surrounded by a cluster of half a dozen fruit trees: lemon, orange, avocado. Whoever had built the place had landscaped it with great loving care. But the present occupants had not done much to preserve either the house or the trees. The two-story building needed paint as badly as the trees needed water and pruning. On several of them, the outer bark had been blasted away where they had been used for rifle practice. No fruit would grow on them again.

Small thing, Bolan thought, as he and April climbed slowly toward the house, but it made him angry anyway. It should not have surprised him, of course. People who had no regard for human life would not fret over a few dead fruit trees. So Bolan was about to give them something to truly fret about.

They heard the second guard before they saw him. He was loping down the dirt driveway, dodging around the half-dozen cars parked there. He gripped a Winchester 1200 Defender shotgun lazily in one hand. He used the other hand to drum out a beat on the fenders of the cars he passed.

"Hey, Ben, you seen my Doors album? I'm getting pissed at having to come to you every time I want to play it, man."

He listened for an answer. Silence. Immediately he swung the 12-gauge into both hands, sweeping it in front of him at hip level. "Ben? You taking a smoke or what?"

When no answer came, he pivoted and bolted back up the driveway, legs pumping and arms churning so fast for cover he did not think to yell a warning to the others.

He was just spanking around the front fender of a blue Pinto when something huge jumped out at him. White eyes burned intensely from behind a grease-smeared face. Powerful muscles strained beneath skintight black material. The word Armageddon came to mind as he hefted the shotgun to blast the thing away.

But something had a hold of his hair, yanking his head back so sharply he lost his balance. As he struggled to regain his footing, he saw that it was a woman who was tugging his hair. His back was arched backward when he first saw her face. Then he saw the flash of steel in her hand and felt the flaming blade plunging into his heart.

April held the handle tightly, letting the body's falling motion pull itself free from the thick blade. She wiped it clean and handed it back to Bolan.

"That's two," she said.

Bolan studied her a moment. He wanted to hold

her, ask her if she was all right, maybe even stash her safely to the side while he blitzed the damn house alone. But there was no time now for assessing emotions, nor fancy heroics. The odds of success were better with both of them going in. And she had already proven a dozen times on this mission that she could handle herself in the field as well as any of the Stony Man team. The emotional toughening, the ripening, would just have to come in its own time.

"How do you want to do this?" she asked. He recognized the impatience, a side effect of adrenaline.

"You take the front, I'll take the back." He looked at his watch. "Give me five minutes to get into position. The lights in the windows indicate that some of them are upstairs. I'll assume that the rest are in the living room at the front of the house. Once I come blasting through the back, I want you to count to ten. Slowly. That will give everybody upstairs a chance to get down the stairs and head in my direction. Those already downstairs will also be distracted toward me."

"That's when I come in."

"Right. They should all be focused on me, their backs temporarily to you. Come in shooting."

"Except for Royce Banjo."

"If at all possible. You know what he looks like?"

"I do read magazines, Mack," she said.

"Okay, then. You're on." He started to jog away, turned, came to her and pulled her close, and kissed her roughly on the lips. She kissed him back just as roughly, lips grinding with something more than passion between them. He released her and hiked away without a word.

Bolan eased soundlessly through the weeds, then the overgrown yard, until he was pressed flat against the side of the house. He slid along the rough wood, brushing off pieces of chipped paint with his shoulder. His foot touched something and he hesitated. Only a spent shotgun shell, red and gold in the moonlight. A dozen of them lay scattered next to a torn, rusted lawn chair. Under the chair were four crushed cans of Lite beer. Someone had been sitting in the chair swilling brew and shooting at the trees.

Which meant that there were no neighbors close enough to complain about gunshots—either that or they were used to the sound. Good, Bolan thought, because they're about to get an earful.

He had to work fast now. It would only be a matter of minutes before someone inside realized that the guy with the shotgun hadn't come back yet.

He edged along the house, ducking under the shaded windows, working slowly toward the corner. Then there would be a quick swoop around the rear and through the back door. Only this time there were more of them inside than there had been at Byron York's survivalist camp.

But he had April now, armed and ready. He pictured her crouching by the front door, her heart thumping wildly. He tried to force the picture out of his head, but his concern for her had settled deep in his gut already, where it burned like a glowing branding iron. He had already come to accept his own death, but could he ever accept April's?

No time to brood on it now. Not with less than two hours until Sunday. Not with Dante and Zossimov still on the loose....

A window was hefted open in front of Bolan. A man with a red bandanna tied around his curly brown hair stuck his head out. Cupping his hands around his mouth he shouted, "Hey, Ben, tell him where the goddamn Doors album is! Steve—" The curly-haired man with the bandanna turned his head slightly and noticed Bolan pressed against the wall. He opened his mouth to warn the others. Thereby he requested his own doom.

Bolan let the Beretta fulfill the request. A stutter of three bullets drilled into the man's face. The man recoiled backward and his already dead skull bounced into the window. A symphony of broken glass accompanied his collapse.

"Cops!" a woman inside shouted.

"They're shooting at us!"

Bolan could hear the scramble for guns inside. A shotgun blast kicked out the rest of the window above Bolan as he ran for the back door.

"Stay cool! Stay cool!" a woman shouted. "Zack, take the back door. James, you and Tina cover the front. Royce, grab that shotgun and—"

"You bet I will!" Royce Banjo's gravelly voice shouted above the noise.

Bolan did not wait for the troops to be deployed. He planted his feet in front of the flimsy screen door that guarded the back door and started pumping bullets through it. He heard a muffled cry, someone falling.

"Watch out!" the woman screamed. "They're coming in the back."

Bolan urged a couple more rounds through the door before dodging around the side of the house again. He heard a rifle butt knock through the glass window over the kitchen sink, then the explosion of a shotgun firing into the night.

"How many?" the woman demanded.

"Can't see them," someone answered.

"See any cop cars?" Royce roared.

"They're not cops," the woman answered. "Cops would use a bullhorn."

"Then who?"

No answer.

Bolan dropped flat to the ground, pressing close to the side of the house. Five feet ahead was the window through which he had killed the man with the bandanna. Resting on the windowsill was the tip of a rifle barrel. It swiveled back and forth, scraping along the sill, looking for a target.

April had prudently decided not to try and rush the front door. She must be pinned down somewhere, waiting for a sign.

I've got a sign, Bolan thought, plucking an RGD-5 antipersonnel grenade from his webbing. A .69-pound sign with 110 grams of TNT. Better than neon.

He crawled forward on hands and knees until he was directly under the window. He yanked the pin and with a soft hook shot, lobbed the apple-green grenade through the open window.

The man stationed at the window screamed. His yell was drowned 3.2 seconds later by the roaring explosion. Smoke billowed out of the window like a dragon's fiery breath. Amid the smoke, a man's shredded body somersaulted through the air, tumbling to the ground next to his twisted Winchester. His right arm landed ten feet away, near an avocado tree.

"Jesus, I'm hit in the leg!" Royce Banjo hollered from within.

Bolan arose in front of the window frame and sprayed a burst around the room. An Uzi rattled somewhere in the smoke, and the windowsill in front of him disintegrated in a swirl of splinters and dust. Bolan swung away from the window just as more bullets zipped by, rustling a few lemon tree leaves as they took off toward the moon.

"The window!" Royce yelled.

"He's only hitting us one place at a time," the woman shouted back. "I think he's alone."

"Then he's crazy," someone said.

"He's dead!" Royce Banjo spat.

Bolan angled around to the back of the house again and hardballed another RGD-5 grenade through the kitchen window over the sink. The explosion brought another chorus of agonized screams as hot shrapnel peppered the walls. A waterfall of smoke rushed out over the sill of the small window. Bolan heard a man's tortured moans. *"My face! My face!"*

Heavy footsteps rushed toward the back of the house. Bolan dived behind an orange tree as the bullets speared the darkness around him. Bark flew, severed branches dropped around him, dirt clods kicked up into his face. At least five terrorists were firing from the kitchen windows, pinning Bolan facedown in the dirt.

He felt a tug on his sleeve, saw a sudden six-inch tear in the nightsuit, a flash of skin and a thick line of blood growing on the tricep like a red lizard. There was too much adrenaline to feel any pain. That would come later. If there was a later.

A chunk of flying bark nicked his cheek and he covered his eyes. "Now, damn it," he muttered. "Now!"

The monotonous drone of gunfire from the kitchen suddenly had a new voice. It was the angry buzzing of April's Wilkinson Arms Linda, chuffing out 9mm death nuggets in three-round harmony.

Bolan scrambled to his feet and zigzagged across the yard at a 45-degree angle. He fired another couple of bursts from the Beretta in answer to April's Linda. It was the conversation of soldiers, the message as clear as any civilian language: *I'm coming*. Then, with a running jump, he vaulted through the side window. The impact of his fall was broken by the mushy corpse of the man whose face once wore the red bandanna, but Bolan rolled over him and onto his feet in one continuous motion. His Beretta scanned the room.

"Just like a man," April said, ushering in the three survivors at gunpoint. "Letting me do all the cleaning up."

"DAMAGES?"

"Five dead. One dying of internal bleeding. Two wounded, but ambulatory. One wounded and unconscious. Two unwounded."

"Dante?" Bolan asked.

April shook her head. "Not here."

"Okay," Bolan said, satisfied. "Now we can get to work."

One of the prisoners spoke. "What are you going to do?" Bolan recognized her as the woman who had given all the orders earlier. She was in her late thirties, her face thin and harsh. A scratch on her cheek bled slightly.

"I'm asking the questions," Bolan said.

She sneered. "What are you, some kind of renegade cop or something?"

Bolan stood in the middle of the living room amid a haze of drifting smoke and dust, as if he were enveloped in a yellow fog. A charred hand, torn from somebody's body during one of the explosions, lay in the middle of the floor like a lost starfish. Bolan stepped aside to avoid it as he approached the prisoners, all seated in a line against the wall.

Royce Banjo glared at him. "You know who I am, man?" He looked the same as his photographs, the long dark hair braided with brightly colored feathers. He was pressing his hand against the shrapnel wound in his upper thigh.

"We've got nothing to say," the woman said, folding her arms in front of her chest. She shot Royce a tough look. "None of us."

Bolan caught the exchange. She was afraid of what Royce might say. Why? If he was one of them, what were they afraid of?

"Say, Royce," Bolan said, "you weren't really going to play at the festival today, were you?"

"Take us in or kill us," the woman said. "We've got nothing to say."

Bolan looked at her. "For someone with nothing to say, you talk too much."

"It's okay, Lynn," Royce jumped in. "I can handle this cracker."

"Yeah, sure you can, Mr. Banjo," April said, sweeping her weapon gently across the seated line of prisoners. "We just saw how well."

"Now, now," Bolan said. "We mustn't be too hard on Mr. Banjo. He doesn't realize that we saved his life tonight."

"You what?" Royce barked. "How, by fragging my leg?"

"By keeping you from performing at that festival in about twelve hours."

"You're not making any sense."

"No?" Bolan pointed his Beretta at Lynn's worried face. "She knows what I'm talking about. Don't you, cuddles?"

"Screw you!"

"What's he mean, Lynn?" Royce asked her.

"Nothing, Royce. He's trying to divide us, hoping we'll tell him where to find J.D." She stared up at Bolan, her lips twisting into an ugly grin. "But you'll never find him in time. Never!"

Bolan shook his head. "Lynn, you're not telling the whole truth to your buddy, Royce. You forgot to mention how he was supposed to be killed with the others at the festival."

"You're crazy, man!" Royce forced out a laugh.

"Maybe, but then I'm not the one being set up by my Weather Underground buddies."

"Don't listen, Royce," Lynn said. "He's lying."

Bolan stepped closer to Royce Banjo, leaned forward and stared him icily in the eye. "You do know about their plans for the OPON Festival, don't you, Royce?"

"What plans?"

"Plans for a lot of deaths. And since you'd be there at the time, you would be one of the victims."

Angrily Royce tried to get to his feet. The rush of pain to his wounded leg forced him back down, his face creased with pain. "You're a liar, man. They wouldn't try anything like that."

"What do you think the Weather Underground is? A social club?"

"They wouldn't do anything to harm me," Royce said. "I've given a lot of money to them. They're my friends."

Bolan slowly shook his head with contempt. "I don't know which of you is more pathetic, Royce, you or Dante. At least he doesn't kid himself about who he is. He knows he'll do anything, use anybody to get what he wants. But you and your type think you can play at Robin Hood without ever getting caught in the cross fire. Well, your time has come, pal. Dante used you to get across the country and as a pass into the festival. After whatever he's planning is over and the Feds come in to investigate, they'll find there's one roadie that can't be accounted for and they'll come looking for you. But with you dead, he'll be even harder to trace."

Royce looked at Bolan, realization washing over his features.

"He's lying, Royce!" Lynn hissed.

"Shut up, Lynn," Royce said calmly.

She turned to Bolan. "You're wrong, mister. Sure, J.D. planned something, something that would make us a political power again."

"What?" Bolan demanded. "What did he plan?"

"He didn't tell us any details and I wouldn't tell you even if he did. But he swore that only a few would die."

"Only a few would die...." Bolan's dark eyes brooded coldly upon her. "Where's Dante?"

Her voice trembled as she spoke. "I—I don't know."

"She's telling the truth," Royce said wearily. His voice was hollow and defeated. He didn't care anymore. "Dante doesn't confide anything. All I know for sure is that his girl friend picked him up a few hours ago in her Dodge van."

"You stupid son of a bitch!" Lynn snarled. "When I tell Dant—"

Royce snapped his fist into her jaw. The effort caused a great surge of pain in his bleeding thigh, but not as much pain as it caused Lynn. Her jaw shifted out of alignment and her lower lip split, leaking blood down her chin. She cradled her jaw in her hands, making a choking noise as the blood bubbled through her fingers.

The grubby man sitting next to her started to scramble toward Royce, but Bolan waved the barrel of the Beretta at him and shook his head. The man sank back to the floor.

"As I was saying," Royce continued. "The girl's name is Melissa. She has a condo at the marina." He gave the address and laughed bitterly. "I helped pay for that place, too."

"You think they might be there?" April asked anxiously.

He shrugged. "Don't know. But he spends most of his time there. He might have left for the festival already. They both have passes as part of my crew setting up the equipment."

"Is there any way he could smuggle explosives in with your equipment?"

"No. The security people check everything that comes in with special dogs."

"So how does he plan to do it? How will Dante attack half a million people?"

"He'll do it," Lynn managed to mutter, a trace of a smile showing teeth smeared with blood. "And there's nothing you can do to stop him."

"I'll stop him," Bolan promised.

In the back of his mind flickered a desperate thought. What if she's right?

16

"Anything in the bathroom?"

"Nope," April called. "She washes with Ivory, conditions with Breck, brushes with Crest and protects with a diaphragm. But nothing incriminating."

"Figures." Bolan yanked out another drawer from the small dresser and dumped the contents on the unmade water bed. Panties, bras, panty hose. He pawed through them, then angrily swept them onto the floor with the rest of the clothes he had searched.

April returned to the bedroom, her voice soothing. "Maybe we should just go straight to the festival, Mack. It's going to take some time to get there."

"Fine, but what do we do once we're there? Even if we manage to locate and catch Dante, there's still Zossimov to worry about. And we don't have a clue as to where he might be."

"His file says he always has a hand in the final operation."

"That's my point. It's a cinch we'll never get Dante to tell us anything, even if we take him alive. So where will that put us? And the half a million people at the festival?''

She walked closer to him, laid a warm hand on his arm. ''What exactly is going down at that festival, Mack? Those hardcases we took in Laurel Canyon seem to think there's just some grand scare tactic involved. But you're convinced it's much more.''

''I know it's more. There's a saying, 'The easiest mark to con is another con man,' meaning that people who con others for a living think that no one would dare try to con them. That's why they're so easy to take. Same principle here. I don't know how deep Dante is in this whole thing, but I do know that Zossimov wouldn't bother getting involved unless there were a lot of lives at stake. Maybe Dante and his Weather Underground planned it one way, but that's not how it's going down. Not with Zossimov pulling the strings. He'd let them think they have him by the balls, then he'd pull a switch and slam-dunk them into the ground.''

''So Dante is just a fall guy for Zossimov?''

''He doesn't know it but, yeah, that's how it is. And unless we find out how they plan to attack that crowd, there's going to be a long waiting list at a lot of local funeral homes. It's already too late to stop the festival. It would just beg a riot. So our only chance is to head off the hit as it's about to go down.''

Bolan ushered April into the living room. A plate-glass window dominated one whole wall with a magnificent view of Marina Del Ray and its parade of sailboats and cocky bright spinnakers.

"Expensive view," April noted.

"Paid for from celebrity donations and by robbing banks."

"Why do they do it, people like Royce and the others? They've got everything they worked for, fame and fortune and all that. What can they possibly hope to achieve by linking up with the Weather Underground?"

"Scary, huh?" Bolan said. "But I don't think there's any complicated psychological reason. Some do it for kicks, like that soap star, what's-her-name...."

"Carly Carlyle."

"A woman like her just needed the excitement, the kinky danger. And Dolph Connors, *former* center for the Steelers, he wasn't much different. Didn't want to be thought of as just a dumb jock, so he hung around with what he thought were intellectuals. They paid the price."

"What about Royce Banjo?"

"Yeah, good ole Royce. Born William Joseph Royce in the slums of Atlanta. He's a little different. I think he felt guilty about all the money he'd made, tried to give some back in some way. He's an idiot. He never thought it through."

April pressed her face against the cool glass window, watched a young couple casting off the lines from their sleek cabin cruiser. For a moment she imagined it was her and Mack on that boat, heading out into the early-morning sun. Away from this place, away from their awesome responsibilities. She turned from the window, back to business. "Where does that leave us?"

"It leaves us with no choice but to get down to San Bernadino Valley and start searching. Hal has an APB out on the blue Dodge van and its license number. I wish I could find—" He broke off in the middle of his sentence, and faced the far wall. Under the Fritz Scholder print was a tall chrome-and-glass unit that shelved a Toshiba stereo and speakers, a nineteen-inch RCA tv, and a JVC video cassette recorder. Two of the shelves were lined with video cassettes. Bolan pulled them down one at a time and read the labels. *"The French Connection, M*A*S*H...."* He stopped reading them aloud, tossing the ones he examined onto the floor.

"What are you looking for, Mack?"

"I don't know. But all these people seem to be heavily into video equipment. Maybe they use it like a notebook or a diary, to record current information."

April kneeled, began reading the labels of another shelf of tapes. *"Debbie Does Dallas, Sex Machine.* These are the good ones."

"Here we are, try these," Bolan said, pulling down two cassettes. "These aren't marked."

April clicked on the tv, set the VCR, popped in the first tape. The picture rolled twice, then stabilized. Dan Rather's familiar face ballooned onto the screen, his voice heavy with authority.

"Like Woodstock a generation ago, and the US

Festival the past couple years, OPON is trying to do something politicians and religious leaders have failed to do for years: unite people of all ages and beliefs. Their secret weapon? Music.'' The screen throbbed with writhing bodies of young people dancing, then showed elderly couples with their arms around each other, children of all races playing tag in a grassy field. The camera cut to a close-up of Kris Kristofferson singing on stage. The camera pulled back in an aerial shot of the hundreds of thousands of people as Dan Rather's voice continued. ''And if these crowds are any indication, they might just pull it off.''

The rest of the tape was filled with more local and national newscasts concerning the upcoming OPON Festival.

Bolan slid in the second tape. More of the same.

''What do you think this is for?'' April asked as they watched.

''Blueprinting. This material helps them anticipate what might happen, gives them a scale of probabilities. Helps them to plan better whatever it is they're going to do.''

''But *what*?''

Bolan shook his head. ''That's the five-hundred-thousand-person question.''

They watched more of the tapes. An interview with Leonard Zeno, boy genius, wealthy film director and sponsor. A feature about a day in the life of a soft drink vendor at entertainment events. More aerial shots of rock-festival crowds. Segments filmed under a rotating stage where electronic equipment was stored. Planes skytyping over crowds, announcing the names of groups in giant white letters. Statistics on how many bathrooms are needed at a massive outdoor event, how many day-care centers, emergency medical treatment tents. Everything was presented to show how sanitary and safe such an event can be.

The third tape was a whole episode of "Entertainment Tonight" devoted to following the performers around before, during and after their shows. Desperate groupies, appreciative fans, pushy managers. A camera caught an unidentified man wielding drum sticks, staggering drunk up some stage stairs.

Bolan reached out and punched the Stop button. He grabbed April under the arm and half-dragged her toward the door.

"Mack, what is it?"

"I know how they're going to do it," he said hoarsely, his jaw clenched. "And it's worse than we thought."

IT WAS a matter of common sense. To a soldier, that means combat sense. Mack Bolan, who lived waist-deep in the flowing river of blood that had long been prophesied as his destined route—that sticky swirl daily threatening to pull him into its flow of faceless mangled bodies, a miasma of great gaping wounds, a river that groaned with the muted symphony of violent dying—Mack Bolan knew about combat sense. Indeed, it was the most vital sense he possessed.

Tuned and organized combat awareness told him how the hit was going to go down. The flexing of his survival instincts, plus some prodding from the strongly conditioned retentive web of his combat consciousness, combined to reveal to him the method of the strike.

The secret would be the *transmitter*.... Every unrevealed event needed a method of transmission. The transmitter would be the key element.

Exactly what was to be transmitted was a different matter. The information about that came to Bolan by empirical logic. He figured out the range of possibilites and selected the one that he himself, if he had been the aggressor, would have chosen. Such a method was a mark of respect for the bloody determination of his enemy.

17

"Nothing can go wrong."

She nodded, trying to smooth the worried wrinkles from her brow. "I know."

"Trust me," Dante said, gently stroking her arm.

"I do. I really do."

"Good."

"I guess I'm just a worrier."

His fingers stopped caressing her arm and clamped tightly around it instead, pinching the soft pale skin. His face twitched with sudden rage. "Then keep your goddamn worrying to yourself. It's making me nervous."

"Sure, okay, J.D. Okay." She tried to yank her arm free but he held tight, squeezing even harder. Finally, with a harsh laugh, he released her. She stumbled across the van, massaging her bruised arm.

Dante bent over a box of equipment as if nothing had happened. "Grab that thing, would you?"

Melissa waded through the boxes of electronic devices she couldn't name and picked up a heavy metal box. "This?"

He glanced over his shoulder. "Yeah. Hang on to it a sec."

"What is it?"

"What do you care? Just do what I tell you." Dante stopped fussing in one of the boxes, pulled up the right leg of his jeans, shifted the Colt .45 M-1911 wedged into his boot and scratched his calf. "Damn thing itches like hell. Giving me a rash."

"I can carry the gun for you in my purse," Melissa offered, anxious to get back in his good graces.

Dante stood up, his head bent slightly because of the van's low ceiling. He wore an amused but cruel smile. "Listen, baby, I don't mind making it with you occasionally, but I would never, *never* trust you with my gun. You savvy?"

Melissa lowered her head, swallowed. "Sure, J.D., I understand."

"You'd better. We're not playing house here, lady. We're getting ready to shout a message to the whole *TV Guide* middle-class world outside. Not a message, a goddamn *demand*!"

She listened to his angry voice echoing off the metal walls of the van like a ricocheting bullet. She watched the unnatural light shimmering in his eyes, the clenched fist jabbing the air for emphasis. And she knew why she had always done what he'd wanted, always would. He had the power, he was a mover. If only her smug chairman-of-the-university-history-department father could see her now, could know the physical abuse she'd taken at Dante's hands, could know the emotional and sexual humiliation she'd gladly endured. Know the people she'd killed, snitches she'd offed at his command. Know that she'd do it all again just to be with Dante. That would show him, show them all. And after today, they'd know her for the first time.

Dante finished his speech, his eyes glazing slightly as they stared off through the metal roof of the van as if studying some distant constellation. He took a deep breath, rolled his neck, smiled. "Let's go, baby. The show must go on."

They exited from the rear of the van, their arms full of equipment. Quickly, without looking around, they walked from the special parking lot for performers toward the rear entrance of the stage. Melissa lagged a few steps behind Dante, trying to balance the heavy metal box while she ran to catch up.

Dante looked at her over his shoulder and smiled. "If you drop that, lover, I'll put a bullet through your tiny brain."

BOLAN PASSED THE BINOCULARS to April and pointed. "There. See them?"

"Yeah. Lugging some equipment."

"Right."

She lowered the binoculars, looked at Bolan. "That equipment is part of it?"

"He's got a transmitter in there to signal Zossimov, and some kind of timer to give him time to get out before the holocaust starts."

"Then we have to stop that transmitter,' April said. "And Dante."

Bolan stared straight ahead. "Dante first, then Zossimov."

"Right."

"And one other thing." He turned to look her in the eyes. "No more prisoners."

April nodded. "Okay."

"JESUS, IT'S HUGE," Melissa said, looking around the room, the metal box still clutched to her chest.

They were standing under the stage now, not just an ordinary stage but a giant platform that rotated slowly so the performers would eventually face the entire audience encircling them. The expense of this device had been minimal, compared with the added number of tickets they had been able to sell because of it.

The foundation for the stage was the building Dante and Melissa were standing in now. The stage was fifteen feet overhead and they could hear Willie Nelson above them singing "If You've Got the Money I've Got the Time." The music shook the walls, sprinkling dust like a light mist throughout the room. In the center of the place, mammoth gears strained against each other to keep the stage overhead slowly turning.

Dante snapped his fingers. "Bring that thing over here, Minnie Pearl."

Melissa handed him the metal box. "What's this all for, J.D.? Aren't you ever going to tell me?"

"You'll know the details in—" he looked at his watch "—less than an hour. By then the whole world will know. Meantime, get your ass back in the van and wait for me."

"How long will it take?" she asked nervously.

"You worrying again?"

"No, no, J.D., I'm not worrying. Just, you know, curious."

He laughed. "Just get that blue monstrosity started. I'll be out in a coupla minutes. And have our gate passes ready. Once I've rigged this baby, we want to get the hell out of here as soon as possible. When Zossimov gets the signal, it's going down. Like I said, nothing can stop it now."

APRIL SLAPPED HER PALM into the base of the clip, driving it up into the Linda's checkered plastic grip. Even when firmly anchored, the clip protruded a few inches from the bottom of the grip. That extra few inches allowed the clip to house its full 31 rounds, plenty to do her part of the job. April curled one hand around the handle, cupped the other under the fat maple forehand grip attached to the underbelly of the barrel. "Ready," she said.

Bolan peered through the binoculars, his head swiveling with the moving quarry. "She's heading back toward the van...she's climbing in...she's starting it up. Okay, that's it."

Bolan kicked open the door of the Camaro. It was the best they could rent at the Ontario airport when they flew in from Los Angeles an hour and a half ago.

Security passes to the concert site had been pre-arranged by Hal Brognola. Now Bolan and April Rose were in the midst of the music. So was Dante. The time had come.

Bolan had exchanged his blacksuit for less conspicuous garb: chinos and a bulky blue V-neck sweater. The Beretta 93-R was tucked into his waistband, covered by the baggy shirt.

Once outside the car, they had to shout to be heard. Amplifiers blared from the nearby stage as well as from dozens of other strategically placed amplifiers among the crowd.

Bolan looked around at the hundreds of thousands of people spreading over the surrounding valley like a field of daisies.

There must be more than half a million already there and still more cramming into the gates and scouring the already full parking lots.

As he shifted the Beretta's handle for easier access, one thought flashed in his mind: he had never seen so many smiling, happy people in one place before.

Under other circumstances it would have warmed him, maybe he would even have joined in, clapping hands and singing with Willie. But not now. Not yet.

"Go get her," he shouted to April above the hammering chords of the guitars. "Remember, we don't want her contacting anybody else."

April nodded, ran off toward the van, her gun weighing down her shoulder bag.

Bolan jogged toward the door that he had seen Dante enter. Above him, Willie Nelson picked out a melody. The hollering fans almost drowned out Willie's voice, but he smiled out at them, his wrinkled eyes twinkling in the bright noon sun.

There were no windows, no other doors to the foundation beneath the stage. One way in, one way out.

Bolan gripped the doorknob with his left hand. He could feel the vibrations of the music through the doorknob as he gently turned it. His right hand eased the Beretta out from his waistband. He inched the door open, felt the rush of cool foul air escaping from the crack, took a deep lungful of air and went through the door like a man entering hell.

The first shot sounded before he'd closed the door behind him.

MELISSA PUMPED THE ACCELERATOR NERVOUSLY, feeling some comfort in the roar of the engine. She tapped the heavy gold ring on her finger against the steering wheel in time with Willie Nelson's song, occasionally joining in on a verse, then forgetting the words.

She squirmed on the hot vinyl seat, too agitated to sit still. She knew people were going to die here today, though J.D. had said it wouldn't be many. Mostly people would just get sick, clogging hospitals and scaring the hell out of everybody. Still, some would die; it couldn't be helped. Melissa stared out through the windshield at the happy, singing crowd and tried to determine which ones would soon be dead.

She caught a movement in the mirror on the passenger side. Nothing special, a pretty woman, some way off, striding toward the van. There were plenty of pretty women here today. Still, there was something about that face that made her nervous. A certain determination, a sense of purpose. Like a cop's.

Melissa reached under the seat and pulled out a Walther P-38, the same one she'd used to blow a hole through the guts of the clerk when they'd robbed a 7-Eleven last month. She checked the clip; it was fully loaded with eight rounds of 9mm parabellum cartridges. She leaned to check both side mirrors again. No one there.

Maybe nothing, she thought. But this was no time to take any chances.

She applied the parking brake, climbed out of her seat and moved to the rear of the van. She unlocked the back doors, pushing one open a crack so anyone outside could see it was unlocked. Then she scrambled back into the cool depths of the van, squatted down with her shoulders pressed against the back of the driver's seat, her gun gripped in both hands and pointing at the rear doors of the van.

"Come and get it, bitch," she muttered.

APRIL MOVED QUICKLY, her face purposely intense to ward off some of the roadies who were checking her out.

This close to the stage the throbbing music from the amplifiers created a kind of insistent draft, nudging at her back as she walked. And the hundreds of thousands of feet stomping in time with the music sent a tremor through the ground. The experience was almost intoxicating.

She closed in on the back of the van, her right hand dipping into the purse, finding the comfortable weight of the Linda.

April noticed the rear doors were slightly ajar, probably an oversight when they'd unloaded that equipment earlier.

Her right hand was still wrist-deep in the shoulder bag, aiming the gun ahead of her as her left hand reached for the rear door of the van.

BOLAN WAS ROLLING ACROSS the rough concrete floor, inhaling lungfuls of dust as he spun.

Dante's .45 slug had kicked a chunk of wood out of the doorjamb, but the pounding beat of the music and echo of the amplifiers drowned the sound of the gunshot. They could blast away at each other in there and no one would notice.

That was fine with Bolan.

He stopped rolling once he had angled the stack of reserve amplifiers between himself and Dante. Another bullet ripped through one of the amplifiers, and the impact sent it toppling to the floor.

Bolan had the Beretta set on single shot. He didn't want to risk a three-shot burst ramming through a weak spot in a wall and flying out into the crowd. One bullet at a time, yeah, just make each one count.

"Hey," Bolan called out, "what the hell are you doing? I'm just here to check the damn gear for the stage."

"Don't screw with me, buddy," Dante shouted. "This thing gets checked once in the morning and once at night. I know. Now, who are you?"

Well, it had been worth a try. Bolan let his mind play back the photo it took of Dante's location when he'd come through the door. Adjusting it according to where the voice was, Bolan popped up from behind the amplifiers.

The Beretta flung death toward Dante, but the revolutionary had already ducked behind one of the giant rotating gears that turned the platform overhead. The bullet pinged harmlessly off the vertical metal rod of the drive shaft.

"Okay, you want to play rough." Dante's voice was pinched with fear.

He's already set the timer, Bolan realized. *Unless it's stopped, the transmitter will send its signal. The massacre will begin.*

Bolan ran out from behind the amplifiers, desperate to secure a better shooting angle.

Dante stood, both fists gripping the M-1911, but it was a rushed shot. The bullet sank soundlessly into a pile of wooden fence posts stacked behind the moving target.

Bolan knew Dante was panicked, trying to kill Bolan and still get out before the transmitter kicked in. "Goddamn it, fight me, you bastard!" Dante screamed in desperation.

Bolan stepped out from behind the spare benches, the Beretta hanging at his side. "You just got your wish, guy."

MELISSA'S FINGER FLEXED around the trigger, taking up any slack. She waited for the door to open, giving J.D. every extra second to get back. Her hands were steady as her eyes focused down the barrel. She held her breath.

Waited.

Waited.

Waited.

Nothing happened. No one pulled the door open. No one came after her. She sighed, smiled. "Paranoid," she said to herself as she stood up. Seeing cops everywhere, shit. "Getting as bad as J.D."

She turned toward the front of the van, left hand on the back of the driver's seat, right hand loosely holding the Walther.

She cursed.

Directly in front of the van stood April, the yawning muzzle of her oversized gun hovering a couple inches from the windshield. It was aimed at Melissa's chest.

April stood in a professional shooter's stance, eyes unwavering from her target. Her skin tingled at the sight of the Walther P-38 dangling from Melissa's right hand, knowing how close she came to having its hungry load buried in her body. But

April had learned from the best, Mack Bolan. Learned not to trust anything so easy as an open door. As her hand had reached out for the chrome latch, she'd played back a mental tape of Dante and Melissa climbing out of the van. She saw the look of contempt on Dante's face as he'd watched Melissa's clumsy exit from the back of the van; saw him slam the door behind her, causing Melissa to jump slightly. Saw him give it that extra jiggle to make sure it was locked.

"Drop the gun, Melissa. It's your only chance to live."

From the back of one of the trucks a man shouted at April. "Hey, lady, what the hell do you think you're doin' with that?"

He was joined by several others. She overheard one say he was going for a security guard.

April ignored them, concentrated on what she was doing. "Drop it, Melissa. *Now!*"

But Melissa just stared into April's eyes, a tiny smirk tugging at the corner of her mouth. And April knew what was going to happen next.

Melissa swung the gun up, dropping into a crouch at the same time.

April squeezed the trigger. The bullet punched through the windshield, leaving a clean hole behind it, then punched through Melissa Stowe's chest. The entry hole was as clean as the one in the windshield, but the exit wound sprayed a thick sauce of blood out between her shoulder blades, freckling the blue walls of the van. The impact lifted her off her feet, banging her head into the roof, then dropping her dead body on the floor.

Only those near the van knew something had happened. The amplified music continued to wash through the crowd, an acoustic balm, the performers and audience alike oblivious to the bloody drama at their feet.

April didn't bother checking the body, she ran for the door where she'd last seen Mack.

"YOU'RE DEAD, MAN," Dante grinned as he stood up and squeezed the trigger.

There was nothing heroic in Bolan's decision. It was a calculated risk based on the facts of the situation.

Fact one: the transmitter's timer had already been set, so whatever he did he had to do fast.

Fact two: Dante knew the timer was set, and he was scared. He was long-term panicked.

Conclusion: due to the time element, the situation had to be forced now. The only way to force it, considering they both had strong cover, was to bring Dante out for a clear shot. The only way to do that was give *him* a clear shot.

Bolan's edge: Dante's dumb reaction. A reaction born of panic.

Bolan waited until the last possible moment, studying Dante's face for the sign. The sign would tell him exactly when Dante intended to pull the trigger.

Dante, imperceptibly but undeniably, gave the

sign. He pressed his lips together, as people do at that precise moment when intent turns to action.

Bolan lunged forward onto the ground and brought the Beretta up and in alignment with Dante's chest.

The fanatic's bullet whizzed inches by Bolan's head. It nicked the edge of a green bench.

The 9mm ace of spades Bolan dealt to Dante chopped off a chunk of Dante's right shoulder, whirling the guy around. The Colt catapulted from his hand, clattering into some bales of barbed wire.

Dante reeled backward over the low concrete wall built around the giant gears. The sleeve of his left hand was snagged by one of the gear's teeth, pinning it between tooth and cog.

Dante's hand was trapped, the gears grinding slowly around, each turn tugging the sleeve tighter.

"Can the timer be shut off or is it booby-trapped?" Bolan called as he climbed to his feet.

"Screw around with it and find out."

Bolan nodded at the gears. "In less than a minute, it'll be your hand in there."

The door opened. Sunlight split through the semidarkness. Bolan spun.

"It's me," April called.

"You okay?"

"Yeah."

"Melissa?"

"Secured." The word came out flat and toneless. Bolan knew what she meant by that. No prisoners.

Dante screamed. The gear had tugged his little finger into the cog. The heavy metal teeth were grinding it to pulp. His legs buckled from the pain, but still the gear pulled him along.

Overhead Willie Nelson and Waylon Jennings sang "Mamas Don't Let Your Babies Grow Up to Be Cowboys." The crowd sang along, almost louder than the two performers at the microphones.

Sweat blossomed across Dante's twisted face. The gear ground another notch and another finger was chewed off his hand.

Bolan walked over to the transmitter, looked it over. The timer was inside; there was no way to know how much time they had. There was no way to know if the whole damn thing was boobytrapped against tampering. Bolan turned back toward Dante. "Any chance of you telling me about this thing or about Zossimov?"

Dante's lips curled back into a rabid snarl. "Not a chance in hell, scum. You and that piece of skirt can—"

Bolan's shot flew into Dante's churning mouth, ripped off a flap of lower lip, shattered four incisors, continued drilling through the throat, then chipped the spinal column and finally burst through the base of skull.

The second shot followed almost the same trajectory.

Blood lathered from Dante's mangled mouth,

dripping red strings. He sagged to his knees. He was dead. But even in death the giant gears would not release him. They kept on dragging him around in a slow circle, grinding off bits of his body.

"What about the transmitter?" April asked, staring wide-eyed at Bolan. It was an effort of will to keep her voice crisp and efficient.

"It's probably rigged. Try to alter it and it'll blow. That in itself would probably be a secondary signal."

"So what do we do? If you're right about their plan...."

"That leaves us with only one thing we can do now," Bolan said, looking at the door. "We have to race against the signal to Zossimov, and we have to win the race."

18

"Mr. St. John? Hey, Mr. St. John!"

Zossimov turned to face the man walking toward him. "Yes?"

"We've got to be going soon if we're gonna keep on schedule. We do have a couple other jobs to do today."

"Of course you do, Mr. Simms," Zossimov smiled, his accent very proper, very British. Somehow that seemed to impress Americans. "And on behalf of the OPON Festival, we appreciate your indulgence. It is just that timing is so important here. Press and media coverage, you know. Can't live with them, can't live without them, eh?" He chuckled, dabbed a white handkerchief at the corners of his mouth.

Simms nodded pleasantly. He dug his hands deep into the pockets of his blue flight suit. "Okay, Mr. St. John. You're the boss. But it had better be soon."

"Good man, Simms. And of course your transmitters are properly adjusted?"

"Yes, sir. Just as you asked. We're waiting for that signal and we'll use it to home in on when we fly overhead." He tugged the bill of his blue cap nervously. "But I tell you, Mr. St. John, me and the boys have been flying these rigs for a lot of years. We know what we're doing without any homing device. It's totally unnecessary."

Zossimov winked. "I couldn't agree more, sir. But you know how it is trying to convince the brass to try something new. They want guarantees that are absolute. Nothing can go wrong."

Simms bristled. "Skytyping is not that new anymore. Hell, we've been doing it for years for some of the biggest corporations in the country. Coors Beer, Datsun, Ford, even the Army, Navy and Marines. Nobody's ever tried to tell us our business before."

"And no one's trying to do it now, Mr. Simms. To be perfectly honest, sir, the extra money I've paid you to install the special transmitter comes out of my own pocket. Helping to organize this OPON Festival is my biggest job yet in America, and if I pull it off, I'm hoping I'll get enough employment from it to stay here permanently. You can see why I'm especially nervous, yes?"

Simms nodded sympathetically. "Sure. I didn't know. Still, Skytypers Inc. are the only ones in the country who do this, and we're damn good at it. We know when and where to release our chemical compound. Jeez, Mr. St. John, your message will be more than one thousand feet tall and six miles long. So don't worry. People will be able to see it for about four hundred square miles."

"I just want the crowd at the festival to see it," said the Russian.

"They'll have the best view of all. We'll be right smack over them. Can't miss."

Zossimov smiled. "Perfect."

"Yeah, but we do have to take off soon. There's so much air traffic over the festival that they've got their own control tower. And there's strict FAA regulations about—"

"Yes, yes, I'm certain," Zossimov interrupted impatiently. He checked his watch. "I suggest you get your pilots prepared. If the signal doesn't come within five minutes, take off without it. Satisfactory?"

"Yes, sir. That'll do." Simms touched his finger to his cap bill and walked back to the office where his pilots were waiting.

Zossimov allowed his smug grin to inch across his face. It was almost over. Within minutes the five North American SNJ-4 Navy training planes would be airborne and on their way to dump a payload of agony and death on half a million people.

Of course the pilots knew nothing about it. They thought they were doing what they were paid to do, skytype a message of welcome to the audience at the festival. Five planes flying in precise formation, releasing their special cloud-making compound at computerized intervals, puffing out letters more than 1,000 feet tall and 75 feet wide: white letters taller than the Empire State Building. A 20-character message would span six miles. Six hundred fifty dollars was the usual rate for this kind of job, but Zossimov had paid them four times that to make sure everything went right. Especially to have them install the transmitter-receiver in the lead plane, the one with the controlling computer. Simms imagined "St. John" was just a fussy character anxious about his job, so he'd agreed. What the American did not know was that once the planes flew within a certain range of the transmitter that Dante had set off, the computer controls would lock, releasing the contents of the planes' tanks. And there would be no way manually to stop it.

Of course, the simple "smoke" solution that they normally used for their messages had been replaced last night by two of Zossimov's agents. The new solution was much more complicated and would have a decidedly more extreme result than a mere message in the sky. More extreme even than what J.D. Dante had planned.

The pathetically naive radical thought the planes would spray a highly diluted chemical solution similar to Agent Orange. The result would have been mass illness and a few hundred deaths of those susceptible to respiratory ailments. Babies, old people, those already suffering from breathing problems.

A shortsighted plan.

Zossimov's compound, specially developed by expert Soviet chemists, would have a much more devastating result. Only part of that result would be the belated realization by Zossimov's enemies that the KGB was undoubtedly the most murderous organization operating today—and that, increasingly, the KGB was everywhere. The big result would be that some very heavy stuff fell from the sky and burned a bunch of civilians all to hell.

Simple process, really. Usually the skytype solution is injected into the plane's exhaust manifold, where it is steamed and compressed. From there it is forced through a ten-foot pipe bolted to the right wing of the plane. When the solution hits the cold air, the white puff is formed that makes up the letters.

But Zossimov's formula changed that.

Instead of harmless white smoke dots, virtual time bombs that fall fast would be planted across the sky.

The altered solution contained the aluminum salt formed when mixing naphthenic and aliphatic carboxylic acids. Combined with a stabilizing compound, the mixture was a napalmlike substance completely harmless until the exhaust manifold evaporated the stabilizing additive.

Once the mixture began to condense, it formed heavy clumps that would fall to earth. The warmer temperatures would cause the sleet-size globs to self-ignite as they fell.

The result: a rainstorm of sticky drops of fire.

Napalm rain.

Whatever each drop hit, it would cling to until it had burned itself out. By which time the damage would have been done.

Zossimov wished he could be flying one of the planes himself so he could watch the fireballs pelting the screaming mass of panicked people. *Right now they are hypnotized by their own humanity, loving each other as they love the whining music they listen to. But within a few minutes they'll be trampling to death that same neighbor they're singing with now.*

Zossimov rubbed his hands together and muttered, "Beautiful."

By the time the holocaust was sorted out by authorities, he would be across the country, dining with the Soviet ambassador. But first he would meet with his "partner" Dante. Of course, he would have to kill the rude young man. Leave some incriminating evidence. That way the police would be happy, the press would be happy and his own bosses would be happy. And Zossimov, in his new office at 2 Dzerzhinsky Square, would be happiest of them all.

Meantime, Dante and thousands of people who attended the festival would be dead. Thousands more would be horribly mutilated, their bodies burned and scoured by a fire they could not extinguish.

"Mr. St. John!" Simms waved from the tiny building where he and his pilots were waiting. He jogged over to Zossimov. "The signal. We just picked up your friend's signal. They're ready for us."

"Wonderful. Go ahead."

"Yes, sir." Simms, a short powerfully built man with a black mustache, smiled. "Been looking forward to this all day. My wife and two-year-old daughter are at the festival. It's going to be the first time my daughter sees me in action. She's never seen what I do."

Zossimov grinned. "I'm sure she'll never forget it."

"Yes, sir. I hope you're right." Simms half-saluted, turned and jogged back to the other four pilots.

Sentimental idiots, Zossimov thought, shaking his head in contempt. It would have been so much easier if he could have bribed this fellow Simms. But these American pilots fairly bristled with integrity and pride. Well, let's see how they feel once they discover what they have done, he thought. As he watched the five pilots walk briskly toward their planes, Zossimov felt his own heart trip-hammering against his ribs.

A rain of fire. If only he could be up there to see it himself. Ah, well, he'd have to content himself with watching it on the news tonight. *If* any of the cameras or crews survived the flames.

Nothing more to do here, he sighed, waving at the pilots as he headed toward his car. Soon it would all be history. And like most history, it would be written in blood.

"There, Mack! Over there!" April yelled.

Bolan jammed the accelerator to the floor and spun the car off the narrow side street that ran the length of the tiny private airport. He aimed the car at the chain link fence. The Camaro fishtailed, streaking the pavement with a rooster tail of black rubber.

"Head down," Bolan ordered as the car straightened out and rammed the fence, ripping it off a post. The sharp jutting edges of metal scraped the car's roof and fenders. The noise inside the Camaro was intense as the car tore through the fence.

A hundred yards down the runway sat five red-and-white single-engine planes. Bolan recognized the type, used mostly as training planes for Navy and Marine pilots during World War II. And he knew the 650-horsepower Pratt & Whitney radial engines could wing them at about 210 miles per hour flat out.

Five pilots in blue flight uniforms were wildly waving their arms at him, gesturing him off the runway. But Bolan continued tear-assing toward them.

"Get their attention," he said to April.

She leaned out of the window and fired a burst from the Linda.

The five pilots ran back to the building, diving through the door to safety.

Bolan nodded. "That ought to keep them out of the way for a while."

"You see Zossimov?"

"Not yet."

"Maybe he left already."

"No way," Bolan said above the engine whine. "He's a perfectionist. He'd hang around until they were up in the air. He didn't get his reputation by being sloppy at the last minute.''

"See that parking lot on the other side of the hangar?" April pointed ahead of them to the left. "Let's try there.''

Bolan roared toward the walled lot, then jumped on the brakes, wrestling the car to a halt at the corner nearest the hangar. Their doors were already flying open before the car had stopped.

April rested the Linda on the top edge of the low cement wall, scanning the near-empty parking lot. Bolan leaped atop the hood of the Camaro for a better look. With one hand shading his eyes and the other clutching the Beretta, he scrutinized the parking lot for movement or cubbyholes to hide.

"Unless he's lying under one of those four cars, he's not there.'' Bolan hopped down from the hood and started for the small building where the pilots were. April fell in step next to him.

"At least we stopped them from taking off,'' she said.

"I want him,'' Bolan said, letting his icy eyes bore into hers. "No prisoners, and no escapes.''

As they approached the building, Simms's voice called out to them. "I'm warning you two. I've just called the police. They'll be here within minutes. You'd do well to haul ass out of here.''

"Don't worry, guy,'' Bolan replied, tucking the Beretta back into his waistband and holding up his hands. "We're not outlaws and we're not here to hurt you. We're looking for a guy named Fyodor Zossimov."

Simms voice was wary. "Don't know any Zossimov."

"He's probably using another name. Tall, thin, distinguished looking, graying at the temples."

"You mean Mr. St. John. Guy from the OPON Festival that hired us. He was just here a second.... *Hey!*"

Fifty feet down the runway the lead plane's engine shook and grumbled, the propeller twirling in an almost invisible circle. The plane began to roll.

In the pilot's seat sat Fyodor Zossimov.

The cockpit canopy was still open. Zossimov expertly poked and prodded the controls.

"Stop! Stop!" Simms called as he bolted after his plane.

Zossimov twisted suddenly in his seat, his hand pointing a Tokarev TT-33. It bucked twice in his hand and Simms doubled over, clutching his chest.

April opened fire immediately. Slugs chipped away ineffectively at the old training plane's fuselage.

The plane turned onto the longer runway and began to pick up speed.

Bolan had already made his choice, perhaps even before they'd arrived at the tiny rural airport. He had made it back in Melissa Stowe's apartment after watching the videotapes, when he first realized the skytyping planes were the key. It was the only logical way they could affect so many people at once. And maybe he knew then that it would have to end here.

He hiked up the left pant leg of his chinos and yanked free the clip he had taped to his leg. The pain from pulling the tape was sharp but short. Expertly Bolan ejected the old clip from the Beretta and slammed in the new one. He dropped to one knee and aimed, swiveling the gun so it tracked the forward movement of the plane. He swung the gun ahead of the plane, anticipating its path.

And waited.

When the fuselage and its 180 gallons of fuel crossed his sights, he squeezed the trigger.

The special tracer bullet, with its column of pyrotechnic composition in the base, flashed through the air on a jet stream of its own making before it rammed through the fuselage.

But the plane kept rolling, picking up speed. Bolan squeezed the trigger again, twice.

Two more smoky white lines appeared. The second tracer bullet ignited the fuel supply.

The front end of the plane bucked off the ground from the explosion, sending the propeller spinning off on a solo flight without the rest of the airplane. It soared harmlessly through the air, bounced on the runway, spun some more, came to rest in sparks and screeches on the asphalt.

Flames whooshed around the cockpit as Zossimov scrambled out, jumping down to the right wing.

Bolan and April silently lifted their guns and aimed.

The second explosion boomed before they had a chance to pull the triggers. A tornado of flames whirled around the plane, splashing thick burning globs around the runway.

Napalm. KGB style.

And in the middle of the fiery tornado, Fyodor Zossimov's Savile Row suit ignited. He batted frantically at the flames as he tumbled off the edge of the wing onto the pavement. He rolled himself on the ground, trying to smother the greasy fire. But the flames would not die.

As he watched, Bolan saw what had been in store for the half-million people singing and celebrating less than twenty miles away.

As he beat at the flames on his body, Zossimov's hands suddenly ignited, too.

A flame licked at his head and his hair was immediately alive with fire.

He screamed, began running toward Bolan and April and the four pilots gathered around their dead buddy.

He held his burning arms away from his sides as he ran, like a giant blackbird with flaming wings.

Bolan lifted his gun to end it, but April gently pushed the barrel aside.

"Let justice run its course," she said. "It doesn't get the chance often enough."

He deferred to her, was resigned to accepting the liberty April had taken of him. He lowered the Beretta.

April Rose had dived deep into the caldron of boiling hellfire this mission. Therefore he encouraged her true caring and compassion to speak its terrible price. Zossimov burned.

They stood and watched as the flapping, charred bird, consumed by hungry flames, stumbled toward them, fell, crawled a couple inches, then collapsed. Zossimov's body continued to twitch in agony as the flames devoured what was left.

No Phoenix would ever rise from those ashes.

Would that the whole KGB burned so completely....

19

"What's in the package?" Hal Brognola asked as he entered the room.

"A present," April said.

"For me?"

Bolan shook his head. "Nope. For your niece. A graduation present." He slid it across the table.

The Fed clamped his cigar between his teeth and picked up the box, jiggled it slightly. "What is it?"

"A tennis sweater with 'OPON Festival' stitched discreetly on the sleeve."

"Hey, terrific," he beamed. "She'll love it. She did nothing but nag my sister about not being able to go. You sure you got the right size?"

"You've shown us enough photos to have a good idea."

"Well, what's the point of being an uncle if you can't brag?"

April's face radiated relief, determination, calmness. "Go ahead and brag all you want, Hal. Someday she'll be bragging about you."

"Maybe." A wide smile creased his face.

They could hear the gentle patter of Virginia rain outside.

"How long's this weather supposed to last?" Bolan asked.

"Day or two," Brognola answered, settling into a chair. "Why, is it interfering with your California tan?"

"I guess I prefer it to the Weatherman's forecast," Bolan said. "For heavy violence."

Brognola flicked a thick ash from his cigar. "At least Zossimov won't be back." He furrowed his brow and looked at April. "How's that wound of yours?"

"Fine. Only hurts when I do handsprings."

Brognola looked at Mack. "What kind of shape are you in, Mack?"

"I've been hurting since the Paradise mission in Colorado. My leg's all messed up. Usual stuff."

"You two did fine out there," Hal said, wishing he had the command of language to be able to read out and grant peace to these warriors, to mend them and sustain them. "Damn fine, the both of you."

He pushed himself to his feet and departed, leaving the two of them alone.

Bolan looked at April a minute before speaking. "You did do a hell of a job. He's damn right."

"I don't feel like I did. I can see all the mistakes I made."

Bolan nodded. "It's a feeling that goes with the job. It never gets any better."

"What ever does?"

"The world, maybe. With a little help."

She went to him, leaned over his chair and kissed him firmly on the mouth.

With lips still pressing tightly against hers, Bolan eased her over the arm of the chair and into his lap. Overhead he could hear the rain tiptoeing across the roof. He could smell her distinctive sweet scent, feel her soft cheek brushing against his rough skin.

She pulled back, her fingers caressing his face.

"This is the right stuff," he said, grinning.

"What stuff?"

He kissed her again before answering. "The stuff dreams are made of."

"I like it," she laughed.

HE'S EXPLOSIVE. HE'S MACK BOLAN... AGAINST ALL ODDS

He learned his deadly skills in Vietnam...then put them to good use by destroying the Mafia in a blazing one-man war. Now **Mack Bolan** is back to battle new threats to freedom—and he's recruited some high-powered forces to help...**Able Team**—Bolan's famous Death Squad from the Mafia wars—now reborn to tackle urban savagery too vicious for regular law enforcement. And **Phoenix Force**—five extraordinary warriors handpicked by Bolan to fight the dirtiest of anti-terrorist wars around the world.

Fight alongside these three courageous forces for freedom in all-new, pulse-pounding action-adventure novels! Travel to the jungles of South America, the scorching sands of the Sahara desert, and the desolate mountains of Turkey. And feel the pressure and excitement building page after page, with non-stop action that keeps you enthralled until the explosive conclusion! Yes, Mack Bolan and his combat teams are living large...and they'll fight against all odds to protect our way of life!

Now you can have all the new Executioner novels delivered right to your home!

You won't want to miss a single one of these exciting new action-adventures. And you don't have to! Just fill out and mail the card at right, and we'll enter your name in the Executioner home subscription plan. You'll then receive four brand-new action-packed books in the Executioner series every other month, delivered right to your home! You'll get two **Mack Bolan** novels, one **Able Team** book and one **Phoenix Force**. No need to worry about sellouts at the bookstore...you'll receive the latest books by mail as soon as they come off the presses. That's four enthralling action novels every other month, featuring all three of the exciting series included in the Executioner library. Mail the card today to start your adventure.

FREE! Mack Bolan bumper sticker.

When we receive your card we'll send your four explosive Executioner novels and, absolutely FREE, a Mack Bolan "Live Large" bumper sticker! This large, colorful bumper sticker will look great on your car, your bulletin board, or anywhere else you want people to know that you like to "live large." And you are under no obligation to buy anything—because your first four books come on a 10-day free trial! If you're not thrilled with these four exciting books, just return them to us and you'll owe nothing. The bumper sticker is yours to keep, FREE!

Don't miss a single one of these thrilling novels...mail the card now, while you're thinking about it. And get the Mack Bolan bumper sticker FREE as our gift!

HE'S UNSTOPPABLE. AND HE'LL FIGHT TO DEFEND FREEDOM!

FREE! MACK BOLAN BUMPER STICKER
when you join our home subscription plan.

Gold Eagle Reader Service, a Division of Worldwide Library
2504 W. Southern Avenue, Tempe AZ 85282

YES, please send me my first four Executioner novels, and include my FREE Mack Bolan bumper sticker as a gift. These first four books are mine to examine free for 10 days. If I am not entirely satisfied with these books, I will return them within 10 days and owe nothing. If I decide to keep these novels, I will pay just $1.95 per book (total $7.80). I will then receive the four new Executioner novels every other month as soon as they come off the presses, and will be billed the same low price of $7.80 per shipment. I understand that each shipment will contain two Mack Bolan novels, one Able Team and one Phoenix Force. There are no shipping and handling or any other hidden charges. I may cancel this arrangement at any time, and the bumper sticker is mine to keep as a FREE gift, even if I do not buy any additional books.

166-CIM-PABM

Name	(please print)	
Address		Apt No.
City	State	Zip
Signature	(If under 18, parent or guardian must sign.)	

This offer limited to one order per household. We reserve the right to exercise discretion in granting membership. If price changes are necessary, you will be notified. Offer expires April 30, 1984.

GET THIS MACK BOLAN BUMPER STICKER FREE!

See exciting details inside.

Don Pendleton on

MACK BOLAN

Since the early days of Mack Bolan's war against the Mafia, I've relied on the skills of a team of "scholars of organized crime" to keep The Executioner series factually accurate and to meet the growing demand for my books. Now the team includes a handpicked corps of writers.

I've chosen men like Ray Obstfeld whose novel *Dead Heat* was nominated for the Edgar Award for our kind of fiction. I trust Ray in the same way Mack trusts the personnel of Able Team and Phoenix Force. I believe he's bested himself with *Flesh Wounds*. In these back pages, I'll continue to introduce members of my team during the exciting future developments in Mack's career.

Here's just a hint of what's to come.... The whole Stony Man program is jeopardized by the twisted workings of the Western intelligence bureaucracies. Phoenix Force and Able Team continue the fight under the president's sanction, but warrior Mack Bolan goes further and further into the cold to confront the KGB's worldwide strategy-of-terror head-on.

Mack stays hard. But like the old days when he soloed against the mob, hard alone is not enough. The Executioner will need all his savvy, all his instincts, all his hard-won experience and honed reflexes to stay alive—and winning—in a war without backup. Enjoy him!

—*Don Pendleton*

MACK BOLAN

THE EXECUTIONER 58

appears again in
Ambush on Blood River

A soldier-for-hire named Scarr led a troop of Cubans back into the darkest heart of Africa. Scarr and his band of renegade mercs, under the control of the KGB, had returned to retrieve a fortune buried there by mercenaries years before.

The stolen hoard contained not only riches but damning documents that could ignite global horror. Mack Bolan had to snuff Scarr fast.

For this mission in the savage land of Blood River, The Executioner flanked himself with one of the deadliest forces known to modern man....

Bolan flies with Phoenix Force!

Available wherever paperbacks are sold.

MACK BOLAN

THE EXECUTIONER SERIES

I am not their judge, I am their judgment—I am their executioner.
— *Mack Bolan,
a.k.a. Col. John Phoenix*

Mack Bolan is the free world's leading force in the new Terrorist Wars, defying all terrorists and destroying them piece by piece, using his Vietnam-trained tactics and knowledge of jungle warfare. Bolan's new war is the most exciting series ever to explode into print. You won't want to miss a single word. Start your collection now!

"Today's hottest books for men.... The Executioner series is the grandest of all!"

— *The New York Times*

GOLD EAGLE

Mack Bolan's
PHOENIX FORCE
AN EXECUTIONER SERIES
by Gar Wilson

Phoenix Force is The Executioner's five-man army that blazes through the dirtiest of encounters. Like commandos who fight for the love of battle and the righteous unfolding of the logic of war, Bolan's five hardasses make mincemeat out of their enemies. Catch up on the whole series now!

"Strong-willed and true. Gold Eagle Books are making history. Full of adventure, daring and action!"
—*Marketing Bestsellers*

#1 **Argentine Deadline**   #5 **The Fury Bombs**
#2 **Guerilla Games**   #6 **White Hell**
#3 **Atlantic Scramble**   #7 **Dragon's Kill**
#4 **Tigers of Justice**

Phoenix Force titles are available wherever paperbacks are sold.

GOLD EAGLE

Mack Bolan's

ABLE TEAM

AN EXECUTIONER SERIES

by Dick Stivers

In the fire-raking tradition of The Executioner, Able Team's Carl Lyons, Pol Blancanales and Gadgets Schwarz are the three hotshots who avenge terror with screaming silvered fury. They are the Death Squad reborn, and their long-awaited adventures are the best thing to happen since the Mack Bolan and the Phoenix Force series. Collect them all! They are classics of their kind! Do not miss these titles!

"This guy has a fertile mind and a great eye for detail. Dick Stivers is brilliant!"

—*Don Pendleton*

#1 Tower of Terror   #5 Cairo Countdown
#2 The Hostaged Island   #6 Warlord of Azatlan
#3 Texas Showdown   #7 Justice by Fire
#4 Amazon Slaughter

Able Team titles are available
wherever paperbacks are sold.

GOLD
EAGLE

HE'S EXPLOSIVE.
HE'S UNSTOPPABLE.
HE'S MACK BOLAN!

He learned his deadly skills in Vietnam...then put them to use by destroying the Mafia in a blazing one-man war. Now **Mack Bolan** is back to battle new threats to freedom. the enemies of justice and democracy—and he's recruited some high-powered combat teams to help. **Able Team**—Bolan's famous Death Squad, now reborn to tackle urban savagery too vicious for regular law enforcement. And **Phoenix Force**—five extraordinary warriors handpicked by Bolan to fight the dirtiest of anti-terrorist wars around the world.

Fight alongside these three courageous forces for freedom in all-new, pulse-pounding action-adventure novels! Travel to the jungles of South America. the scorching sands of the Sahara and the desolate mountains of Turkey. And feel the pressure and excitement building page after page. with nonstop action that keeps you enthralled until the explosive conclusion! Yes. Mack Bolan and his combat teams are living large...and they'll fight against all odds to protect our way of life!

Now you can have all the new Executioner novels delivered right to your home!

You won't want to miss a single one of these exciting new action-adventures. And you don't have to! Just fill out and mail the coupon following and we'll enter your name in the Executioner home subscription plan. You'll then receive our brand-new action-packed books in the Executioner series every other month, delivered right to your home! You'll get two **Mack Bolan** novels. one **Able Team** and one **Phoenix Force**. No need to worry about sellouts at the bookstore...you'll receive the latest books by mail as soon as they come off the presses. That's four enthralling action novels every other month, featuring all three of the exciting series included in The Executioner library. Mail the card today to start your adventure.

FREE! Mack Bolan bumper sticker.

When we receive your card we'll send your four explosive Executioner novels and, absolutely FREE, a Mack Bolan "Live Large" bumper sticker! This large. colorful bumper sticker will look great on your car. your bulletin board. or anywhere else you want people to know that you like to "Live Large." And you are under no obligation to buy anything—because your first four books come on a 10-day free trial! If you're not thrilled with these four exciting books. just return them to us and you'll owe nothing. The bumper sticker is yours to keep. FREE!

Don't miss a single one of these thrilling novels   mail the card now. while you're thinking about it. And get the Mack Bolan bumper sticker FREE!

BOLAN FIGHTS AGAINST ALL ODDS TO DEFEND FREEDOM!

Mail this coupon today!

Gold Eagle Reader Service, a division of Worldwide Library
In U.S.A.: 2504 W. Southern Avenue, Tempe, Arizona 85282
In Canada: 649 Ontario Street, Stratford, Ontario N5A 6W2

FREE! MACK BOLAN BUMPER STICKER
when you join our home subscription plan.

YES. please send me my first four Executioner novels. and include my FREE
Mack Bolan bumper sticker as a gift. These first four books are mine to examine free for
10 days. If I am not entirely satisfied with these books. I will return them within 10 days
and owe nothing. If I decide to keep these novels. I will pay just $1.95 per book (total
$7.80). I will then receive the four new Executioner novels every other month as soon
as they come off the presses. and will be billed the same low price of $7.80 per ship-
ment. I understand that each shipment will contain two Mack Bolan novels. one Able
Team and one Phoenix Force. There are no shipping and handling or any other hidden
charges. I may cancel this arrangement at any time. and the bumper sticker is mine to
keep as a FREE gift. even if I do not buy any additional books.

NAME _____ (PLEASE PRINT)

ADDRESS _____ APT. NC

CITY _____ STATE/PROV. _____ ZIP/POSTAL CODI

Signature _____ (If under 18. parent or guardian must sign.)

This offer limited to one order per household. We reserve the right to exercise discretion in
granting membership. If price changes are necessary. you will be notified.
Offer expires 29 February 1984.   166-BPM-PACM